To Holly

Dead Sexy

Cameo MacPherson

Rose and Pestle Publishing

CMR

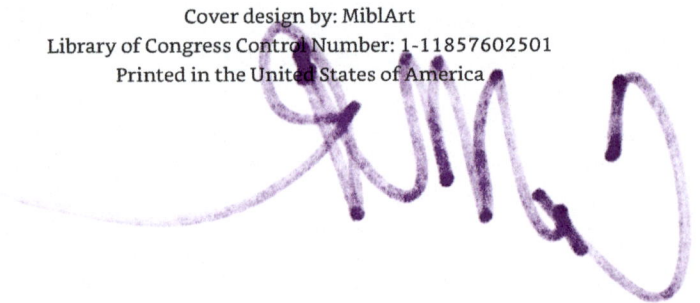

Contents

Chapter One

As he reached out to embrace her, a tidal wave of heat swept over Cassie. Her skin flushed with color and her eyes darkened with passion as his muscular thighs strained beneath her, rocking her back and forth. Her hands clenched tightly around his shoulders, pinning him to the ground so she could take control.

As she forced the undead creature back into his grave, he began to weaken. His arms fell away, relinquishing their strangle hold on her neck, and the frantic bucking of his legs ceased as the consecrated soil leached the life away from him. She held him down until he was completely drained, making sure there was nothing left in him to rise again.

Once she was sure he was permanently dead, she stood up, her long legs unfolding until she was at her full five feet and nine inches. Using the spikes of her stiletto boots for added purchase, she climbed out of the grave, pulling herself up with the ease of a body designed by the dubious gifts of the Cataclysm. Pushing the crimson tumble of her hair away from where it had fallen across her face, she surveyed the now-quiet cemetery with an ever-increasing sense of dread.

"Shit," she said, brushing soil off of her skintight leather pants. "Why do all my dates have to turn out this way?"

Earlier

Being a zombie hunter wasn't a bad gig. It paid well, and there was never a shortage of employment. Benefits were pretty good, too. Full dental, not to mention paid holidays to exotic locations. So what if those exotic locations always ended up being dark and haunted moors instead of bright Caribbean beaches? With her skin, Cassie wasn't much for the beach scene, anyway. She had a tendency to burn faster than a vampire caught in a tanning bed.

She had hunted vampires for a while, but that had turned out to be literally a dead-end job. Ever since the reformation acts had passed, vampires were considered an endangered species. Now, even if you managed to find one, the only thing you could do was send it to one of the underground sanctuaries that protected vampires from the general populace.

And where was the fun in that?

She supposed she could have gotten more work chasing down ghouls or goblins, but her heart just wasn't in it. They were too easy, and frankly, too messy. You wouldn't believe what demon blood could do to leather. She had ruined at least three pairs of custom-designed boots before she got out of that field.

That left fairies, unicorns, and werewolves. Fairies were too irritating, unicorns were too damned virginal, and werewolves had full human rights 27 days a month... with a few additional rights the rest of the time.

Not to mention that her best friend Ash was a were'.

Any way you looked at it, hunting zombies was her best bet. Especially when you factored in the perks - and one of those perks was sitting in her office right now.

Long wavy black hair pulled back by a rough cord tied at the top of his neck... dark chocolate eyes set in a face sculpted by Michelangelo... and the muscles to match.

Gorgeous muscles. Mouth-watering muscles. The kind of muscles that made the palms of Cassie's hands start to itch and her fingers tingle with the need to run them across his shoulders and down his back to his equally well-honed ass.

"So exactly who is it you want me to track down?" Cassie asked, doing her best to ignore the lascivious suggestions her subconscious was whispering in her ear.

It wasn't easy. The moment David MacDuff had walked through the front door of Jones's Post-Mortem Tracking Agency, Cassie had been struck by the way his presence had filled her office. The air had seemed to thicken, carrying with it the promise of a fierce summer storm and making it hard for her to breathe.

It wasn't just his classic Roman features that

made him so compelling. Sure, high cheekbones combined with a killer jaw line, aquiline nose, and - heaven help her – the tiniest hint of a cleft in his chin certainly didn't hurt his appeal. But there was something intangibly erotic about him, a magnetism that drew Cassie in like a mothman to a flame.

She knew she would end up getting burned, but she couldn't help dreaming about the heat they would generate in the meantime.

With a determined effort, she shoved her fantasies back into her subconscious where they belonged. There was no point in imagining the impossible. Besides, any guy who looked like that was bound to be taken already. Speaking of which...

"You don't want me to hunt down your girlfriend, do you?" she asked, fixing him with her most intimidating glare. "Because you should know it costs extra to track a woman."

Male zombies could usually be counted on to follow habitual patterns of behavior, but the females of the species were devious as hell. They would fight till their last bartered breath was gone.

Cass respected that. That's why she charged more to take them down.

Her prospective client's face was earnest as his gaze locked onto Cassie's, his eyes darkening until it felt like he was trying to stare into her soul.

"No, it's not my girlfriend – I don't have one." He hesitated before continuing with a self-deprecating laugh, "I guess the right woman never found me."

At his words, Cassie felt an unaccustomed flush

of warmth spread through her. "That's good," she managed to answer. "It'll make things easier."

You bet it will make things easier. It means he's single.

Yes, he's single, Cass reminded herself, and we're cursed. Cursed with a capital C.

Nine years ago, due to an unfortunate confrontation with an unhappy wizard, she'd become the recipient of a 100 percent bona fide malevolent curse. From that day on, any man she fell for was destined to betray her and break her heart.

So what? It's not like we want to marry this guy – just get to know him. Preferably in the biblical manner.

I've given up on men, Cass told herself. There's no point in trying.

No point? You did see his ass, didn't you?

Ignoring the traitorous voice, Cassie attempted to continue the interview. "Mr. MacDuff…"

"Please, call me David. All my friends do." As he spoke, he leaned forward, causing the neck of his shirt to gap open just enough to reveal the top of a chest tantalizingly smooth and tanned.

It was enough to make her mouth go dry.

"Look, Mr. MacDuff, my caseload is pretty full and I don't have time to waste. Why exactly are you here?"

A look of distress flitted over his features as he shifted uneasily in the chair.

"It's my brother, Gideon." His voice lowered to a whisper, as if saying the words out loud would be too painful. "He died in a car accident."

"Tell me about it," Cassie said in her most professional voice, fighting the urge to reach out and brush his arm as he spoke.

"He came back a few months ago." A faint smile softened the firm line of his lips. "It was like we had been granted a miracle. We were so happy to see him." The smile turned bitter, hardening into a pained grimace. "But it wasn't long before I started noticing things that seemed... wrong. I'm not sure what came back, but it wasn't my brother. It wasn't the Gideon I knew."

It never was. Zombies were born from a combination of overwhelming determination and the magic latent in the air since the Cataclysm had happened a few decades ago. Technically, anybody could come back as a zombie, but most people chose not to. The price was too steep. For every stolen breath - every second of reanimation - they traded a piece of their life force, a piece of their soul, if you want to call it that. If they lived long enough, they would end up nothing but puppets operated by the darker forces of magic.

That's where people like Cassie came in.

"He's gone, isn't he?" David asked. "Gideon never really returned." Sorrow and anger shifted the cast of his features, giving him a stronger, more ferocious expression that went straight to Cassie's heart.

Damn, this was the last thing she needed.

I mean, yeah, she could use the money. She had an image to maintain, and metal-studded bodices and

Italian silk didn't exactly come cheap. Plus, there was that sports car she had her eye on. It would look absolutely wicked with the new sunglasses she had bought, matching them perfectly.

But the money wasn't worth it - not if she had to deal with Mr. Sex Bomb here to get it.

She'd just have to pass on this one.

"I'm sorry, Mr. MacDuff, I'm not going to be able to help you." She stood up and held out her hand, anxious to get him out of the office before she could do anything stupid. "I just don't have the time to do justice to your brother's case."

"Please," he interrupted, ignoring her outstretched hand. "I know you're considered the best in the business..."

"What do you mean I'm *considered* the best?" she muttered. "I *am* the best."

"... but that's not why I came all this way," he continued. "They say you're fast, that you can find an undead before he even suspects you're hunting him."

"They're right. I can."

"That's why I'm here." David's eyes lit with determination, burning like a wildfire dangerously close to spreading out of control.

Fighting the temptation to break out some marshmallows and chocolate and sit back to enjoy the show, Cassie opened the top drawer of her desk and pulled out an assortment of business cards.

"I can give you the names of some very reliable associates of mine..." She slid the cards across the desktop, careful to avoid any physical contact with him.

He stared at the cards for a moment. "You want me to hire someone else?" He shook his head in a slow, deliberate act of defiance. "No."

"Excuse me?" No one told Cassie no. *No one.* "What did you just say?"

"I said no." His voice was low and rough as his hand moved to the cards and shoved them decisively away. "I want you. Only you."

Cassie's heart flipped over in her chest, filling her with an unfamiliar sense of longing. David MacDuff was bad news; she had known it from the start. She had to get rid of him now.

For her sake, and for his.

Unfortunately, he didn't give her a chance to interrupt.

"I need you to find Gideon,' he continued, "and I need you to do it quickly. I'm willing to pay anything you want to make sure that happens."

Against her will, a spark of curiosity shot through Cassie. *Willing to pay anything? Why is he so desperate?*

She sat down. "You're awfully anxious. Why? Do you have something against zombies in general, or is it just your brother?"

David shook his head again. "Something brought Gideon back. Maybe if I knew what it was, I could help him... maybe even get him back to the way he was before the accident." His hands clenched, and she could see him struggling to force the next words out. "But if he really has changed, if he's not in control of his actions anymore, I want to make sure he finds his final rest. And I want someone who will do it as swiftly and painlessly as possible."

He looked at her, his eyes brimming with pain. "Can you do that? Can you make sure he won't suffer?"

"No, I can't." It was bad business to lie to your clients. It made them hesitant to pay the tab when it finally came due.

"Then there's no hope for him?" The color drained from his expression, leaving him looking pale and vulnerable.

"I'm not saying that." Against her better judgment, Cassie found herself wanting to soften the blow. If her instincts were right, and they usually were, David MacDuff cared deeply about his brother Gideon. "There's a slim chance he'll go down easy... if you hire someone who knows what she's doing."

"Which is precisely why I came to you in the first place." He reached across the desk and circled her wrist with his fingers, holding it in a firm but gentle grip.

A fierce heat spread from his touch, reminding her why giving in to his request would be such a colossally bad idea.

Still, it wasn't his fault he caused a major hormonal imbalance to her system. It wouldn't be right to punish him for her over-active libido, would it?

"If I were to take the case, I'd need your assistance," she hedged, half-hoping to scare him off. "It helps to have a family member or a close friend along for the ride." Even after death and rebirth, people - or what passed for them these days - were creatures of habit. Having someone who could identify those habits made her work much easier.

He sat bolt upright, releasing her wrist in his eagerness to agree to her demand. "Anything you want." He raised his face to hers, hope back in full force and shining brightly from his eyes. "Just say the word."

Anything I want? Now that's an intriguing proposition. We'll be stuck together in close quarters. Riding hard and fast in that little blue coupe, sharing late night meals of dim sum and pizza. Maybe, if the mission runs too long, we might have to check into some seedy little five-star hotel for a little rest and... relaxation.

And eventually she'd let her guard down, and everything would go straight to hell.

No, she'd take the case, but she'd find a way to keep her hands off of him. It would be strictly business.

"I'll do it," she said, suspecting she would regret it later. "I'll take the case. And I'll do everything I can to make it painless - for both of you. You have my word on that."

David rose from his seat, moving swiftly around the desk to take her hand in his. "I can't tell you how much it means to me, knowing you'll make it as easy on him as possible. How can I ever thank you?"

She felt the jolt as soon as their hands touched, that quick electric buzz that ran straight up her arm and spread through her body.

Oh yeah, this was going to be hell.

Chapter Two

The problem with people before the Cataclysm was that no one believed in anything. Say what you want about individual belief systems, but it turns out they served a purpose after all. They provided a natural channel for the magic that was present in the world.

Most people weren't aware it existed. There were some people who practiced a sort of ritual magic, but no one expected anything concrete to come of it. The majority of people who did manage to conjure something usually chalked it up to coincidence.

Well, except for the few who called demons. Most of those just died.

Religion was the same. You had groups of people all over the world nominally believing in the same things. Sure, there was the odd report here and there about miracles or apparitions, but in the back of their minds, you wouldn't find many people who truly believed. And when people don't believe in anything, there's no outlet for real magic. Real magic needs a focus point. Something to draw it in, to concentrate and direct it.

By the time the 21st century rolled around, that didn't exist.

Scientists of the time didn't realize it, but with

the void of belief, magic had been building up for years, growing stronger and wilder. Eventually it reached critical mass. The world had stockpiled so much magic, it got to the point where it couldn't hold any more without exploding.

So it did.

The magic shot outward, seeking people who had a kernel of belief in something - in anything - and it turned them into a living reflection of those beliefs.

It was a confusing time, to say the least.

***

Sorting through her wardrobe, Cassie debated the merits of each piece of clothing before deciding if it should go into one of her suitcases or back into the cavernous vault that served as her walk-in closet. Hidden behind Makore wood walls, the vault itself was made of reinforced steel fortified with a couple dozen jinxes, charms, and anti-personnel mines lurking in wait, ready to dispatch any and all intruders suicidal enough to mess with her stuff. It was, without a doubt, the most dangerous room in her house.

A girl had to keep her priorities straight.

"Camisole - yes. Pashmina - yes. Bustier – definitely yes." Zombie hunting was messy enough in itself; there was no reason to make it worse with ugly clothes.

"What about the kimono?" Ash, or Ashley

Kazue Pendleworth-Miller to be precise, held up a short silk robe of jet-black silk shot through with opalescent strands of mother-of-pearl thread.

"Hmm... yes." It would be cold in Scotland this time of year. Of course, it was cold in Scotland any time of year.

Ash laid the robe on the ever-growing pile of yeses. "So, you're telling me this guy owns an actual castle?"

In addition to being Cassie's best friend, Ash was also a were'. She was the daughter of a kitsune - a Japanese fox spirit - and a werewolf, and if that wasn't the strangest pairing that had happened during the Cataclysm years, it was definitely one of the most intriguing.

When she was younger, Cassie had been fascinated by the couple. She had gone so far as to draw up complex scenarios - complete with detailed illustrations - of how exactly the two had ended up together.

Technically Ash was more of a werefox than anything, but whatever she was, you wouldn't want to piss her off during her time off the month... a fact Cassie had been painfully reminded of at the age of sixteen when the full moon had coincided with Ash stumbling across those same graphic drawings of her parents.

Cassie still carried the claw marks from that fight on her arms, but Ash always said it was only fair. She had to carry the sight of sketches of her parents locked in a position even the Kama Sutra didn't know about.

Luckily, the moon was only at a crescent tonight, so Ash was in a good mood.

"So, what is he, some sort of Scottish Lord or something?" she asked, fluffing her short black hair away from her delicate face.

"Nope." Cassie replied brusquely, not wanting to continue that avenue of discussion. The less she thought about David, the better. "Scottish peasant. Well, half-Scottish. I think the other half is Italian."

Ash's hazel eyes narrowed. "But you said he was rich." As far as Cassie's best friend was concerned, if a man wasn't really wealthy, he wasn't really a man. "He must be rich. Otherwise he wouldn't be able to afford the prices you charge."

"Okay," Cassie grudgingly admitted, "so he's a rich peasant. His family bought the castle a couple years after the Cataclysm."

Ash brightened at the news. "That's something, anyway. So what's wrong with him?"

Cassie picked up the kimono, folding it carefully before placing it into one of her rose silk-lined suitcases. "Nothing yet... but give me a couple of days and I'll change that."

"Still no luck on breaking the curse, huh?"

"None."

When they had first realized the curse was real, the two women had come up with a variety of solutions. Voodoo rituals, complicated potions, crystal casting. Nothing had worked. It was always the same. Every time she started to think she might have a chance at a normal relationship, it went to pieces faster than a skeleton on a roller coaster.

She couldn't go through that again.

"Maybe you'll have better luck with this one," Ash said. Unfailingly optimistic, she'd always believed there was some way to break the curse. "There's only one way to know for sure."

"Nope. He's not worth it." Trying to force the memory of David's deep brown eyes out of her mind, Cassie shook her head. "Besides, he may be gorgeous, but he's not my type."

Ash looked up in surprise. "He's dead?"

"Very funny." Cassie threw a tasseled satin pillow at her friend, which Ash easily dodged. "It's worse than that. He's nice."

"Nice, huh?"

"And he's sensitive." She remembered how shaken he'd been as he'd described what he and his family had been going through. "He was really upset over what's happening to his brother."

"Nice *and* sensitive? Oh, the horror."

Cassie refused to acknowledge the sarcasm lurking underneath Ash's words. "Exactly. It's bad enough when I know they're jerks from the start. When they're not, it makes it worse. Like I'm the one responsible for turning them into assholes."

It was the reason she dated the most emotionally unavailable men she could find. She figured if they didn't even pretend to care for her, then it wouldn't hurt as much when they screwed her over.

"Cass..." Ash's voice was quiet. "You know it's

not your fault, right? If they're too stupid to realize what they've got in you..."

"Yeah, yeah, I'm wonderful... I know." And she did know. Most of the time, anyway. "Any guy would be lucky to have me."

"It's true."

"Even if it is, it doesn't matter, because I am not interested in David MacDuff, and I never will be."

"Well then, I guess that means you won't be needing this." Ash grabbed the robe out of the suitcase and balled it up in a tight wad. "I'll just throw it in the hamper."

"Not so fast." Cassie pulled the robe back out of Ash's hands before she could complete her shot. "You know how easily I get cold." She ran her hand over the silken material, soothing out the wrinkles. "And old castles have a tendency to be drafty."

Ashley smirked knowingly, the expression completely at home on her wily face. "I thought so. Poor guy. He won't know what hit him."

***

The drive to the airport wasn't too bad. It took less time to get there than it did to go through the security checkpoints once she arrived. Cassie knew people had complained about air travel P.C. (Pre-Cataclysm), but nothing could compare to how bad it was now.

First there was the standard body scan,

followed by a pat-down to look for concealed weapons. Cassie was wearing her normal travel ensemble – a black bodysuit coupled with form-hugging Egyptian cotton shorts and stiletto heels that slipped on and off easily – and the security guard passed her through with only a cursory frisk.

Next up was the search for concealed magic. The registered wizard on duty, a tired looking half-Sylph woman, pointed Cassie towards an unoccupied pentagram drawn in institutional yellow paint on the concrete floor. Once Cassie was in place, the wizard started the eighteen-step ritual that would detect any hostile enchantments that had been placed on her, as well as detecting residual defensive spells which might interfere with the aircraft's ability to fly.

As usual, Cassie had to produce notarized documentation proving her curse was considered non-life-threatening and sign a waiver stating that, "in the case of it causing the plane to malfunction, she alone would be held responsible for any and all fatalities, injuries, and/or lawsuits."

Once that was completed, she was allowed to proceed to the final step, where she was genetically tested to determine if she was a hybrid which would react adversely to air travel. This was a relatively new step, instituted only last year after three separate incidents of earth elementals (two dwarves and a garden gnome) who went into homicidal rages when they lost contact with the ground.

Finally approved to board, Cassie headed down the corridor the flight attendant directed her to.

Suitcases in each hand, and several wedged under her arms, she struggled to open the door leading to the tarmac.

As she stepped outside, strong winds buffeted her, causing her hair to fly into her face and conceal her vision. When she managed to clear her eyes, the first thing she saw was a sleek Boeing 747-11 VIP, a luxury air cruiser designed for the ultimate in speed and comfort. "MacDuff Industries" was branded in five-foot tall emerald-green letters on its side.

A private jet? I've always wanted to travel in one of those. Could life get any better?

"Thank you for coming. I was worried you'd change your mind." The voice, low and sincere, startled her, and she shifted her gaze to see who had spoken.

It was David.

Busy drooling over the plane, she hadn't paid any attention to his approach, but she couldn't help but notice him now. His hair was pulled back, but this time it was held in place by a silver clip studded with a ruby the color of blood. His shirt - white cotton so soft and silky that it begged to be touched - covered his magnificent arms and shoulders, but the way the fabric draped over them left little to the imagination.

And his legs! Sweet Lord... his legs!

She'd been exposed to men in kilts before – admittedly, some a little more exposed than others - but she had never seen a man wear one as well as David did.

He reached for her luggage. "Let me take those."

As his hand brushed against hers, a shiver coursed through Cassie, starting at the base of her spine and spreading all the way to the tips of her crimson tresses and the bottom of her designer soles. "I'll carry them on board for you."

"Thanks, but I can get them myself." She yanked the suitcases away from him - there was no way she was going to let him within fifty feet of her *or* her baggage.

David smiled a grin that made him look like the boy next door – if you happened to live next door to Mt. Olympus. "Please, it would be my pleasure."

Watching his thighs flex as he bent to pick the bags up, Cassie was pretty sure it would be *her* pleasure.

Or it would have been if she could do anything about it.

"So," she said, trying not to notice as the wind picked up and molded the kilt against his legs in a spectacular display of rampant masculinity, "when does the rest of the crew get here?"

"The crew?"

"You know - the names I gave you. The meta-human migration expert, the ectoplasm analyst, the Feng Shui guy...." Cassie had supplied David with a long list of eminently qualified specialists who formed her usual squad. "Are they already on board?"

"Oh... I forgot to tell you. I didn't call them." He gave a casual shrug which caused his shoulders to ripple in a way that almost made Cassie ignore what he was telling her.

Almost.

"What do you mean, you didn't call them?" She had specifically told him she needed at least four other people for this job. If she didn't have them, it could take weeks longer to track down Gideon.

She didn't have weeks. Hell, with the temptation David was offering, she might not even have days. Or hours.

Struggling not to show her anxiety, she asked, "Why not?"

He gave another shrug, setting those irritatingly distracting muscles dancing again. "My family is working on some pretty sensitive projects. I know I said I wanted this done quickly, but we felt it would be better to limit the number of people involved in the search. It's going to be just you and me."

At her look of dismay, he cocked his head, his deep brown eyes filled with concern. "That won't be a problem, will it?"

A problem? She didn't know which to fear more - working for weeks on end with a man she couldn't let herself be attracted to, or being trapped alone on a plane with him.

"No, no problem at all. Why would it be?"

There was bound to be a pilot, right? Maybe a flight attendant of some kind?

Yeah, but it'd be easy to barricade the door to the passengers' cabin, and I bet the stewardess could be bribed to stay out of our way.

Shut up; he's our client. If our curse gets hold of him, who's going to pay our bill?

While she was busy arguing with herself, David carted the bags up the steps leading into the plane. As the steward, a winged gremlin, carried the luggage inside, David turned back to Cassie.

Standing framed in the doorway, and with the wind pulling at his hair and his kilt, the sight of him was enough to set her heart racing.

"Are you ready to board?" he asked.

No, but what choice do I have?

Resigned to the inevitable, Cassie started the climb up the stairs. "Sure. Lead on."

At least she'd have a nice view on her way to hell.

***

Ten minutes after take-off, Cassie could feel the scream building inside her, growing stronger and stronger until the only way she could prevent its release was to dig her fingernails into the plush fabric of the armrests. Her breath was coming faster and faster as her blood pressure rose, her lungs desperately striving for the oxygen needed to cool her body down.

She was going to kill him.

"Is that better?" David's fingers brushed against the curve of her waist and left a trail of fire in their wake as he adjusted her seat belt.

"Much," Cassie spat through gritted teeth. "You should go back to your seat now."

Right now. Before I spontaneously combust.

"Are you sure it's fastened correctly? We probably won't hit any turbulence at this height, but you shouldn't take any chances." His brows drew down and a furrow etched between them. "It seems okay, but you never know..." He tugged at her belt once more.

How much more of this was she supposed to endure? He was so close she could feel the heat rising from his body... could smell the crisp, clean scent of his cologne threading through her senses and lowering her defenses.

"It's fine."

"Good." He got off his knees and made his way back to his seat. "After all, it is my fault you're short-handed. I feel like I should make it up to you. If there's anything I can do for you..." He stopped as the flight attendant bustled into the cabin carrying a tray heavily loaded with assorted canapés.

Since nibbling on David was definitely out of the question, Cassie settled for grabbing a delicate sliver of pear wrapped in prosciutto and garnished with a sprig of mint and sinking her teeth into that instead.

"There is one thing you could do," she said after accepting a perfectly chilled glass of champagne from the steward.

David leaned forward. "Anything you want. Just say the word and I'll do it. Anything."

As his words reached Cassie's ears, her depraved sub-conscious twisted them, conjuring a picture of him lying next to her in a deliciously decadent bed and whispering the *exact same thing* before moving in to kiss her.

The image felt so real. She would have brushed her hand across her mouth to make sure it wasn't, but she was afraid David would notice her fingers were shaking.

Besides, who wants to find out it's fake, anyway?

She stomped the treacherous thought down. Lust was all right in its place, but Cassie had to remember why she was here.

Shaking her head to clear her mind, she forced herself to focus on reality. "You could fill in some of the details about your brother. You were pretty hazy back at my office."

A flush came over David's skin, warming its olive tone to the color of cinnamon. "I'm sorry. I suppose I didn't want to scare you off before you accepted the job."

The gremlin hovered above them, making sure their refreshments were satisfactory before buzzing back to the cockpit. David waited until he was completely out of sight, and then began again.

"Gideon is – was – my older brother, and the head of MacDuff Industries. When he was killed in a car crash, both the business and the family were thrown into complete chaos."

He paused to take a drink of his soda, and Cassie watched in fascination as a drop of condensation fell from the glass. It landed on his shirt, turning the cloth slightly translucent.

She had to take a quick gulp of her champagne to cool off. This was rapidly becoming a cruel joke.

David set his drink down, the clink of the glass against the table sounding unnaturally loud in the confines of the pressurized cabin. "We were finally starting to get things back under control when Gideon showed up at our door. That was about three months ago."

Three months? That's unusual.

"It took him that long? Usually if someone's going to reanimate, it happens almost immediately."

David hesitated, looking uncomfortable. "Gideon was out of the country when he died." He shifted his gaze away from Cassie, focusing instead on the burnished silver ring he wore on his right hand. Twisting it round his finger, he continued, "We believe it took him that long to make his way back home."

Concentrating on the details of the case, Cassie felt some of her strange obsession with her client recede into the background. It was still there, teasing the edges of her subconscious, but at least it felt more manageable.

"How far out of the country was he?" she asked. "Knowing where he had come from might give me a clue as to why he came back."

"Spain."

Yet another surprise. Spain was an awfully long distance for a zombie to travel. Whatever had driven him to reanimate must have been pretty strong. He would have had to make his way across the

25

English Channel and then find a way to avoid the border checkpoints once he got there. The UK had very stringent supernatural immigration policies, and they would have held him in quarantine until they could be assured he wasn't carrying any diseases which might be a threat to the indigenous Parahuman population.

"Sounds like he was pretty determined to get home."

David nodded. "He was always stubborn. It's what made him such a good businessman. Unlike me," he added. "I've never had the right temperament for the corporate side of the family business. Gideon always used to tell me I wasn't ruthless enough."

She could believe that. David seemed like the kind of guy who would give his last dollar to anyone who spun him a half-believable sob story. She imagined people took advantage of him a lot. He didn't look like a doormat, but she was willing to bet he would lie down and let people do whatever they wanted if he thought it was the polite thing to do.

The kind of guy it would be a crime to inflict her curse on.

Pretending not to notice the disappointment that accompanied the thought, Cassie plowed on. "What is the family business?"

"We do a little bit of everything. Mostly we're known for creating a series of devices designed to assist hybrid species. Have you heard of the Bengsdotter-Hagerman translator?"

"Of course."

Everybody had heard of the Bengsdotter-Hagerman translator. It was a computer program that converted various parahuman languages into English, Spanish, or Japanese, depending on which version you bought. It had helped to bridge the gaps between the new species and to promote mutual understanding.

It was also a heck of a lot of fun at parties.

"My parents helped make it." Cassie could tell he was proud of his parents' accomplishments – there was a warmth in his tone when he spoke of them that would be hard to disguise. "Before the cataclysm, they were both educators. Mom was head of the political science department at the University di Bologna and Dad specialized in bio-chemical technologies. That's how they met."

"What were they after it?" While it wasn't strictly appropriate to ask about a person's lineage in general conversation, he was the one who had brought it up, so she figured it was fair game.

"Mom turned into a valkyrie and Dad became a pixie."

A valkyrie and a pixie? That's almost as intriguing as a werewolf and a kitsune. I'm going to have to get my sketchbook out again.

"Then you're... what? A picyrie? A valkexie?" Maybe that's why he had such a strong effect on her. His parahuman characteristics were obviously making her forget her common sense.

"Human," he said, dashing her theory. "I was born before the Cataclysm. I was three when it happened."

Hmmm. If he was three during the Cataclysm, that meant he was around thirty-one now – five years older than she was. Funny, she would have guessed he was younger.

"You said Gideon was your older brother. That means he's a full human, too, doesn't it?"

"Not exactly," David hedged. "Obviously, he didn't inherit our parents' traits, but even though he was young, he experienced a metamorphosis of his own. He became a berserker."

Cassie whistled through her teeth. No wonder Gideon had managed to make it home. Berserkers were unthinkably single-minded, destroying any obstacles that stood in the path to what they wanted. Make him a zombie, too, and things got radically worse. There was no way Gideon would stop until she figured out what he was after and found a way to give it to him.

Or until she re-killed him.

For his brother's sake, she hoped it would be the first option.

"He never told you why he chose to reanimate?"

"No."

Cassie watched as the memories played over David's face, the melancholic cast in his eyes making him appear especially vulnerable.

"When he first showed up, we didn't think to ask. We didn't care what had brought him back, we were just happy he was there. After the initial shock wore off, I tried to hand the reins of the company back to him. To be honest, I was glad to get out of running it." He began twisting his ring again, seemingly unaware he was doing so. "But Gideon didn't want his job back. He wasn't interested in much of anything about his old life. He wasn't as talkative as he used to be, either. Not that he talked a lot before, but it seemed like after he came back, he didn't want to discuss anything."

That wasn't abnormal for a zombie.

Most people had the wrong idea about the re-animated. They thought zombies couldn't talk. The truth was they didn't *want* to. They were too focused on what had brought them back to life to waste time in meaningless conversations.

"Go on," Cassie urged.

"He started disappearing, and when he would return, he wouldn't even try to give an explanation. Sometimes he'd be gone for days. Usually he'd at least check in with us to let us know he was okay, but about ten days ago, he disappeared completely. I didn't worry about him at first – he's pretty good at taking care of himself – but that all changed last week."

"What happened last week?" She could tell David was having a hard time talking about it, and she didn't want to make this any more painful than it had to be, but she was going to need all the background she could get for this case.

"Two people were camping out near the outer limits of our estate when something attacked them. One of the two was killed, but the other – a woman by the name of Sasha Kramer - managed to make it out alive. She didn't get a good look, but from the little she said..." His voice broke as he continued, "I'm worried it might have been Gideon."

"I'm sorry." Before she could second-guess herself, Cassie reached out and took David's hand. She wasn't about to deny someone a sympathetic touch just because of her damned curse. Besides, just because she felt a little sympathy didn't mean she was in danger of falling for him.

The lights in the cabin flickered briefly.

The pilot's voice came over a discretely hid speaker, informing them of a patch of rough air and advising them to make sure that their seat belts were securely fastened. Shortly thereafter, the steward came out and collected the remains of their drinks and appetizers.

"We're almost home," David said as the steward disappeared back to wherever it was he had come from. "It always gets rough right before we land. But there is one more thing I should let you know." He looked away from her, his face burning a bright red and his shoulders hunched defensively. "I know I should have told you before. I'm sorry I didn't."

Uh-oh. That doesn't sound good.

Cassie held her breath and waited for the stiletto to drop.

David turned to face her, his eyes open and guileless. "The crash that killed my brother wasn't an accident. His car was deliberately tampered with. Some people think I did it."

Chapter Three

When their plane touched down, a stretch limo was waiting for Cassie and David. With sumptuous leather seating, solid walnut appointments, a tastefully muted sound system playing a classical overture, and two holographic TVs, it was supposed to convey its occupants in utmost opulence, allowing them to arrive at their destination in a state of blissful contentment.

Not freaking likely.

He'd lied to her. They'd known each other for less than twenty-four hours and he'd already lied to her. At least now she didn't have to worry about falling for him.

"Have you been to Scotland before?" Seated as far away from Cassie as she had been able to manage, he wore the wary expression of a Tokyo native trying to explain to Godzilla that his house really wasn't the best place to start practicing the monster mash.

"No." She continued to stare out the window, refusing to acknowledge his presence with anything more than the minimum amount of civility required for her to do her job.

At least the scenery was nice. Vast, meandering

roads surrounded on either side by breathtaking vistas of craggy mountains alternating with windswept moors. In the silvery water of a Loch, she could make out the ghostly image of a selkie dancing in the mist.

David tried again. "I think you'll like it. Dad grew up here, so he's a little biased, but Mom fell in love with it, too."

"Is that so?"

Her reply was as unenthusiastic as she could make it, but he didn't seem to get the message. He nodded enthusiastically, a boyish grin lightening his face.

"It is." One corner of his mouth crept further upward, turning his smile hopeful. "If you'd like, I could take you on a tour later. After you get settled in, of course."

She had to give him credit. With the way he was leaning towards her, his eyes sparkling, he managed to make it seem like he cared about her answer.

Too bad Cassie couldn't care less. An abominable snowman had a better chance of buying a summer home in hell than David had of gaining her trust. "No. Absolutely not."

"Oh." He finally seemed to understand there was no point trying to get on her good side. He sat back and didn't say anything else for the rest of the ride.

After what seemed an eternity, Cassie felt the limousine slow.

They were approaching an intimidating set of

gates – looming barriers of twisted metal crowned with menacing spikes and radiating an incandescent glow. Before the limo could stop entirely, the gates swung open. The road curved ahead of them, but as they made their way round the bend, they found their way blocked. Tall trees, allowed to grow unfettered by any human hand, bent so low that their tips brushed the ground. Branches reached out from either side of the road, weaving together to form an impenetrable barrier.

"Shit." She knew she should have left her machete in her carry-on. Now she'd have to get it out of the suitcase in the trunk. She started to unbuckle, but David put his hand on her wrist.

The warmth of his skin startled her, and she felt an oh-so-unwanted thread of desire coil through her at his touch, wrapping her up in a tangled knot of lust and momentarily making her forget she was mad at him.

"Please, allow me," he said, his dark eyes warm and earnest.

She found herself agreeing before she knew what she was doing. "Sure. Whatever you want."

After he withdrew his hand and left the car, sanity came flooding back. Why had she gone along with what he wanted? Even if his goody-two-shoes exterior was belied by his weaselly, treacherous interior, he was still her client. She was supposed to be protecting him.

What was he going to do, anyway? Unless he had a flamethrower hidden under that kilt of his, she didn't know what he was planning on accomplishing.

She watched in dismay as a dryad appeared from her hiding place. Like most wood nymphs, this one was a willowy creature with ivy-green skin allowing her to blend in with the forest, and long chestnut colored hair that rustled in the wind in time with the branches hanging overhead. Her elven features were inscrutable, but she appeared to be watching David intently as he raised his hand in a friendly greeting.

Cassie's heart began to pound as she saw the dryad shift her weight to the balls of her feet. The nymph was preparing for something, but was it for fight or flight?

Before Cassie could warn David of the potential threat, the dryad ran at him in a headlong charge. Cassie wrenched the door open and sprang to her feet, but before she could cross to them, the dryad wrapped her arms around David and rested her face against his chest.

Haltingly, David's arms came up to encircle her, his hands gently patting her back in a familiar manner.

Cassie walked back to the limo, trying to pretend she hadn't leapt from it in the first place. She should have realized there was no threat to David. Dryads were incredibly protective of their territories, and this one obviously considered him her territory.

Slamming the door shut with a resounding thud that they didn't even have the courtesy to notice, Cassie realized she'd never liked dryads. There was something inexplicably nauseating about their behavior.

Especially this one's.

Cassie smiled as she saw David trying to dislodge the girl's arms from around his neck. It looked to be a valiant effort, but his attempts were repeatedly foiled. He was going to have to be a lot more forceful if he wanted to separate himself from the nymph. Cassie was more than happy to assist him with that.

Preferably with a crowbar.

She was heading towards the trunk to get one when the dryad finally relinquished her hold. Feeling slightly disappointed at the lost opportunity, Cassie settled for attempting to eavesdrop on the woman's conversation with David.

Leaning against the limo, she did her best to listen in, but she couldn't hear any of what they were saying. Just as her patience was about to give out completely, forcing her to head for the crowbar after all, David took the dryad's hand and raised it to his lips, brushing a soft kiss over her knuckles.

The dryad shivered, causing the trees around her to tremble and shed a few of their autumnal leaves, and then she stepped out of his path, fading back into the woods and disappearing amongst the foliage.

Don't ask, Cass thought to herself as he came towards her, his strong frame cutting through the air like a sword through Jell-O. You can't trust his answer, anyway. He's already proved he's a liar.

Still... we might need to know for the case...

"So... you two seemed friendly. Is she your girlfriend?"

"Oh. No." He opened the door and held it for her. "Nim works for my family."

She climbed in. "You're sure? You wouldn't be trying to hide anything from me, would you?" she asked as he settled beside her. "Sorry... I meant to say, you wouldn't be trying to hide anything *else* from me?"

David grimaced. "Cassie, I'm sorry. I told you; I thought you might not take the case if you knew."

"Uh-huh. Sure."

The corridor of trees in front of the car parted to let them pass through and then sealed itself behind them after they were safely past.

The castle came into view and Cassie couldn't help but sigh. Sandstone battlements, mellowed by the years into a soft buttery color, flowed into soaring turrets that looked as if they should be holding a princess in wait. Manicured lawns, immaculate and precise, competed with lush gardens and nature walks as to which was more breathtaking. Next to a Victorian style greenhouse, a pond sparkled and shimmered, surrounded by lush azaleas, and unless she missed her guess, there were a few sprites flitting merrily amongst the blossoms.

Well, this just sucks.

She was staying in an actual fairy tale castle, complete with requisite fairies. Too bad she wasn't Cinderella, and David was a far stretch from Prince

Charming.

They pulled up in front of the main entranceway, an imposing structure made up of soaring arches and flying buttresses. Cassie half-expected to see a footman in full livery appear, but to her relief, none showed up. Instead, David leapt out of the car and crossed to Cassie's door, opening it before the chauffeur could. Leaning down, he held his hand out to her.

As Cassie took it, he drew her up until she was standing less than an inch away from him. Her heart skipped a beat as she realized that if she leaned forward just a little bit, she would be able to brush her lips against his. Against her better judgment, her lips parted at the thought, and she found herself reaching to rest her free hand on his shoulder.

His eyes darkened as his body swayed towards hers, and for one crazy moment, she could delude herself into believing he was her prince. Her eyes drifted closed as she leaned in to him, feeling the whisper of his breath on her skin.

"David!" A woman's voice called out, loud and hearty, and he broke away with a look of adoration coming over his face.

"Mom!" He rushed to the side of the woman who had appeared in the doorway and enfolded her in a tight embrace.

Well, that didn't last long. Shortest fantasy ever.

"Mom," David said, drawing back from the hug, "I'd like you to meet Cassie. She's the one I told you about."

As David escorted his mom over, Cassie couldn't help but stare in awe. His mother towered over them both. Cassie suspected that even in her highest heels, she still wouldn't measure up to the other woman.

Her hair, a blonde so pale as to be almost white, was drawn back into a lady-like chignon accentuating her classical bone structure. Her outfit, an elegant day-suit in a cream color, was probably meant to be demure, but it did nothing to disguise the voluptuous curves beneath.

To put it simply, David's mom was built like a brick shithouse.

"It's a pleasure to meet you, Miss Jones. David told me he's confident you'll be able to help us."

"I certainly hope so, ma'am." Cassie meant every word. It was never a good idea to piss off a Valkyrie.

"Please, call me Diana." David's mother drew herself up to her full height, and Cassie could see that she would make one hell of a warrior. Even without the winged helmet and metal breastplate, the woman was intimidating. "I would like this to be over as quickly as possible – for both of my sons' sakes. I'm sure David mentioned people believe he had something to do with Gideon's death."

"Yes." *A day late, but he mentioned it.*

"He didn't." Diana spoke with absolute conviction. "Anyone who knows David knows he could never have done such a terrible thing."

Cassie wasn't so sure about that. Yeah, he looked like he wouldn't hurt a fly, but if there was one thing she had learned, it was that appearances could be deceiving.

David's voice cut into her reverie. "Mom," he said, placing his hand on his mother's elbow to gain her attention, "I'm sure Cassie is tired after her flight."

The other woman looked instantly contrite at the thought her guest might be uncomfortable "Of course, what was I thinking? Come inside and freshen up. When you're ready, I'll introduce you to my husband and the rest of our guests."

"If you don't mind, I'd rather do that now. The sooner we get started, the sooner we can find our answers."

Diana hesitated. "If you're sure...."

Cassie nodded, and Diana led her into the foyer.

The first thing Cassie noticed was the intricately carved wood lining the main staircase and walls, creating an impression of wealth and power. An oil painting - hung in a heavily gilded frame and depicting a traditional hunting scene - dominated the first-floor landing, and other paintings were scattered throughout the room. Their gravitas was lightened by the luxurious arrangements of fresh-cut flowers scattered on tables throughout the room. In front of one particularly impressive bouquet, two men stood with their backs to Cassie. One was a shorter gentleman, - probably no taller than 4'11 - wearing a formal kilt similar to David's, and with bright copper hair and a wiry build.

Combined with the grease stains on his clothes and the residual cloud of magic surrounding him, Cassie was willing to bet he was David's father, the pixie.

Diana went to him, setting her hand on his shoulder in an affectionate manner. "Malcolm, darling, I'm so glad you're here. I thought you'd still be in your workshop."

Malcolm MacDuff turned around. As he saw his wife, his homely face lit up. He swept her into a passionate kiss, dipping her backwards until she was almost parallel to the ground.

How the hell did he do that? She's almost twice his size!

I have absolutely no idea, her subconscious replied, *but we are definitely going to have to start a new sketchbook.*

After the two came up for air, Diana took a few seconds to regain her composure before attempting to finish the introduction. "Malcolm, dear," she said, smoothing her now-rumpled hair, "this is Miss Jones. She's come to help us with Gideon."

"A pleasure to meet you Miss Jones. But then, it's always a pleasure to meet such a lovely young lady." He took Cassie by the shoulders, pulling her down to him and pressing a brief but enthusiastic kiss on each cheek and leaving her flustered.

David's mother continued, oblivious – or maybe just used to – her husband's actions. "And I see we have company."

The other man turned.

If David was a Greek god, then the man before her was pure soldier. Pale green eyes, cold and impersonal, stared out of a roughly hewn face which would never be in danger of being pretty. With a square jaw clenched tightly in rigid masculinity and a slightly crooked nose bordering on jutting, he was the epitome of a military professional... right down to the skull-buzzing crop of his wheat-colored hair.

Diana continued the introductions. "Striker is a close friend of the family. His mother worked with us at university. After she passed away, he spent most of his time with David and Gideon. I've come to think of him as my bonus son." She smiled affectionately as she continued. "He's in charge of security for MacDuff Industries and he served as Gideon's personal bodyguard, so I imagine you two will want to work together."

A flash of heat sparked in Striker's gaze as it flickered over Cassie, examining her from head to toe. "I work better alone," he growled, his inspection pausing momentarily on the dip of her bodysuit's neckline, "but I'm sure we can come to some sort of arrangement."

Cassie felt David stiffen next to her. "Ms. Jones is here at my request, Striker. I expect you to give her all the respect and assistance she deserves."

"Not a problem, boss." The soldier dipped his head, nodding in agreement, but something in the way he moved to Cassie's side and grabbed her above her elbow had her thinking he had his own definition of "assistance" in mind. "I'll make sure she gets everything she wants."

Shit.

One she couldn't trust to keep his hands to

himself, and one she just couldn't trust, period.

It was going to be a long night.

Chapter Four

During the first wave of the Cataclysm, people were caught unaware by the changes taking place. Seemingly ordinary people would go to sleep at night and wake to find themselves transformed into beings out of their dreams.

If only a few had changed, society would most likely have quietly disposed of them and pretended they never existed, but the sheer number of conversions made that impossible.

Some changes were minor. In the back of their minds, most people believed that they were a lot better looking/smarter/more talented than they really were. The magic fulfilled those beliefs, making them "perfect" versions of themselves. There were very few physically unattractive people anymore.

Unattractive personalities were a different matter. Even magic couldn't change that.

Other changes were more radical. Many people transformed into mystical creatures. Mermaids, cyclops, and pixies appeared, along with werewolves, elves, and three different categories of vampires. (Feral, Charismatic, and Sparklers – with Sparklers being the least dangerous but most irritating.) Lesser-known species appeared as well, but in much smaller numbers.

Some of the new species proved to be unstable, and full-humans and meta-humans everywhere banded together for protection and comfort. Those that survived the first turbulent years of the Cataclysm forged a new society based on the idea that anyone who was left must be human at heart.

*Which meant **everyone** was screwed.*

***

It was supposed to be a "family" dinner, a quiet evening consisting of the MacDuffs and those closest to them. In reality, it was a free-for-all.

Cassie took a sip of wine and watched the guests over the rim of her glass. Everyone was talking loudly, and as far as she could tell, there were at least nine different conversations going on.

An impressive feat considering there were only twelve people.

Diana MacDuff sat at the head of the table. Wearing a midnight black evening gown with delicate lace inserts wrapped around her waist, she appeared the epitome of poise and grace, but her voice rang with passion as she debated the ramifications of elite and mass polarization. Her husband sat to her right, cackling with unfettered glee as he engaged in a heated debate of his own - complete with illustrated arguments scribbled on the thick linen napkins – with a man diagonally across the table. Several others ping-ponged between discussions, bouncing back and forth with no apparent attempt at logic or decorum.

Near the middle of the table, Striker was staring into space, surrounded by conversation but making no attempt to join it. He wasn't wearing the MacDuff family tartan, or even a tuxedo like the other male attendees, but the dark suit coat he had on draped well over his muscular form, drawing attention to his broad shoulders.

He didn't seem to be enjoying his surroundings. His eyes were flat and his posture was rigid, as stiff and unyielding as if the dinner was being hosted by Medusa and her sisters. If it hadn't been for the quick flash of desire he'd given Cassie when she'd entered - wearing a little green dress cut up to *here* and down to *there* - she'd have wondered if he was still breathing.

David didn't seem to be having any such problems. He was so engrossed in socializing, she didn't think he'd even noticed she was in the room. But then, why would he? And why should she care if he did? He'd already proved he couldn't be trusted.

Seated towards the far end of the table, he was chatting with the matronly woman at his side, looking perfectly content. He was equally comfortable with the woman on his other side, a scientist who looked to be at least half-siren.

Maybe we should warn her what kind of man he really is...

The siren laughed at something he said, clutching his arm and leaning her upper body against him.

Diana claimed each of the scientists in the room had contributed to the collective efforts of the MacDuff Family's inventions in one way or the other, but judging by the way the siren was batting her eyes at David, the only thing she was contributing to was his ego.

And to think I was worried about hurting him with my curse...

"Excuse me." A cultured English accent cut through her musings. "I couldn't help but notice you seem to have something on your mind. Might I be of assistance?"

She turned to face the speaker.

Charles Wilkinson was a scientist, and apparently a highly esteemed inventor. He held patents for a number of devices Cassie had never heard of, but that had "changed the world beyond all recognition, ushering in a new era of cognitive and perspicacious breakthroughs."

Or so he'd said.

She had to admit, he wasn't bad looking. Dark skin, dark hair gone mostly gray even though he was only in his early forties, pale blue eyes with a scholarly glint accentuated nicely by wire-rimmed glasses, and a trim, well-toned body that hinted at time spent swimming in the castle's temperature-controlled pool.

It's a shame he's such an ass.

Charles was an oddity in this world. He had been old enough during the Cataclysm to undergo a transformation but was one of the few that hadn't done so. He had remained completely and utterly the same, a fact he'd pointed out to her upon first being introduced.

Usually people untouched by the Cataclysm were quiet, colorless people with no belief in anything. Charles was anything but. It was obvious that if he hadn't changed, it was because he thought he was as good as he could possibly get. He was a peculiar mixture of brash superciliousness and social ineptitude.

When she didn't immediately answer his question, he leaned towards her in apparent concern.

"If you're confused by the silverware," he said, drawling the words out in overemphasized solicitude, "I'm sure we can find a spork for you somewhere. That is what you Americans use for most meals, isn't it?"

Hmmm... nice. A cutting insult delivered with only the slightest bite of sarcasm. She had to give him a point for that one. Maybe two since he had provided her a perfect opportunity to get her mind back on the case where it belonged.

She shook her head, smiling ruefully. "I was just thinking how sad it was about our hosts' son. You knew him, didn't you?"

"Gideon?" Charles' eyebrows lifted in surprise. "Yes, I suppose I knew him as well as anyone outside of the immediate family did. We worked together, you know."

"Really?" She had known, but she wanted to keep him talking. According to Diana, Charles had been the primary scientist working with Gideon.

"Oh, yes." He signaled the server to refill his wine. It was easily the fourth or fifth time he had done so. "Of course, I took the lead on the majority of our inventions, but for the sake of his family I allowed them to think he was in charge."

"That was nice of you." And judging from the information she'd already researched, entirely inaccurate. "You must have been good friends."

He took another long drink, draining his glass in seconds. "I always thought so." Staring into the empty cup, he seemed surprised to find it empty. "Where did that wine steward get to?"

Cassie slid her wine over to him. "Were you working on anything in particular before he died?" she asked as he grasped the drink eagerly. "Anything he might have been desperate to finish?"

"Not that I know of," he said between gulps. "We weren't working on any current projects when he died. Why do you ask?" He paused, an uncomfortable look coming over his face as he suddenly recalled what Cassie did for a living. "Oh... I see. You're tracking him, aren't you?"

The rest of the table quieted.

Damn, they must have heard what he said.

The siren next to David gasped, her expression twisting into one of delight and artfully feigned horror. "Are you talking about Gideon? Are you going to kill him?"

Cassie flinched. This was the part of zombie hunting she hated most.

"I don't discuss my cases. Especially not at the

dinner table." Her hosts were going through a hard enough time already. She didn't want to make it worse by shoving harsh reality in their faces.

"Are you going to cut his head off?" the siren continued with a ghoulish glee only someone untouched by tragedy could achieve.

"Lea, stop." David interrupted. His voice sounded calm and polite enough on the surface, but Cassie could hear the message hidden underneath. He wanted the conversation over, and he was going to make sure it ended *now*. "No more of this," he continued, the warm brown of his eyes darkening to a deep charcoal, "You're disturbing Miss Jones."

Ignoring the cold steel beneath his genial disposition, the siren directed a simpering pout in his direction and prattled on. "Nonsense. She does this for a living. It's not like someone like her is going to be upset by a little talk about killing." She giggled, a tinkling sound Cassie suspected would be charming if it came from someone with an ounce of common sense or decency.

Leaning back in his chair, David stared at the siren. "At the risk of being rude," he said, sounding coldly unrepentant, "I suspect someone like *her* knows far more than you about a lot of things. I suspect *she* knows how difficult it is to have no other option but to end someone's life." His gaze sought out Cassie's, and she could read the apology in his dark eyes. "I'm sure it's not something she takes lightly."

"In addition," he added, turning back to the siren, "I'm sure *she* realizes how this conversation will make my parents feel."

With another startled gasp, Lea blanched. "I'm so sorry. I didn't think…" She looked guiltily towards the head of the table.

"It's alright." Mrs. MacDuff's face was pale and her voice sounded strained, but she seemed in control of herself. Her husband reached out and placed his hand on top of hers, and she smiled gratefully before continuing. "Everyone here has been affected by Gideon's death - and by his return. They have a right to know what we're going to do about it."

Cassie couldn't help but feel a wave of admiration for the woman. She was going through what was undoubtedly one of the worst things a parent could ever experience, and she was managing to do so with more grace and composure than could be humanly expected.

It could have been her Valkyrie blood giving her that strength but looking at the way she clung to her husband's hand, Cassie suspected it was something else entirely. Something she'd seen between her own mom and dad, and between Ashley's parents.

Something she'd used to think she might find for herself one day.

Well, she might not be in the running for any happily-ever-afters, but if she had any say in the matter, the MacDuffs were going to have theirs.

"If everything goes right," she said, projecting her most confident and reassuring persona, "I won't have to do much at all. Certainly nothing like what Lea suggested."

"What do you mean?" one of the other scientists - a portly satyr located on Cassie's left - asked.

"Sentient zombies have a reason for coming back. Something they need to do. If that reason is strong enough, it can allow them to retain their minds and personalities until they accomplish whatever it is they came back for. When that happens, they just sort of... slip away. Peacefully."

"It won't hurt him?" Mrs. MacDuff trembled; a quick shiver of motion Cassie wouldn't have noticed if she hadn't been looking directly at the other woman. "You're sure?"

"Yes." Cassie would see to it. "I am."

A laugh full of bravado suddenly shattered the room's stillness.

"Well, I'm sure we don't have anything to worry about," the satyr scientist brayed. "Gideon never did anything without a plan. He must have an excellent reason for coming back."

Others chimed in, echoing the sentiment and choosing to ignore the lingering fear on the faces of David and his parents. Before long, the guests had turned the conversation, steering it away from the unpleasant and moving it in a safer direction.

Unfortunately, not everyone seemed content to let the matter lie. Charles leaned towards her, keeping his voice quiet as he whispered in her ear. "How often do things go right? How many have gone peacefully?"

Out of a hundred? Less than a third.

51

***

In the library after dinner, Cassie went through the stack of papers David's father had left for her. He and Gideon had worked on a lot of projects together, but he couldn't think of anything urgent enough to bring his son back from the dead.

He was hoping Cassie would find something he'd missed.

So far, she was coming up empty. She rifled through the documents, looking for anything out of the ordinary, but she couldn't make heads or tails of the jargon used in them. She slumped back against the backrest of the embroidered chair she was sitting in, accepting temporary defeat.

What she needed was someone who could translate this scientific mumbo-jumbo into some sort of sense. Maybe she should get the Englishman to help. He seemed like the type who would enjoy this sort of thing. Plus, he had worked with Gideon. He might be able to offer additional insight.

A knock on the door caught her attention.

"Come in," she called.

David stood in the archway of the door. "I came to see if you needed anything," he said, wearing a hopeful expression.

It was a good look on him. It made him look trustworthy.

She had to remind herself appearances could lie

– just like he already had.

"I'm fine," she snapped, looking away from him. "You can go about your business."

He came further into the room, ignoring her dismissal. "I wanted to thank you. For the way you handled things at dinner, I mean."

"Don't mention it." *Don't mention anything. Just leave.* "I was only doing my job."

"I don't think so." He shut the door, sealing them in together, and she felt a moment of unease. Suddenly the room seemed too small... too intimate.

"I think it was more than that," he continued, tilting his head and giving her a smile that made her heart skip a beat. "I hired you to track down my brother, not to protect my parents' feelings. But you tried to do so anyway, and I wanted to let you know how grateful I am."

"It was no big deal. Anyone would have done the same."

"But they didn't. You did." His smile broadened, and a rush of warmth flooded over Cassie.

Damn it. She knew he was a liar, why couldn't she convince her hormones of it?

"Whatever." Desperate for a distraction from her traitorous libido, she held up the stack of documents that had been frustrating her. "Do you have any idea what these mean?"

He reached to take them, leafing through them briefly before shaking his head. "I'm sorry. I wish I could be more help, but I didn't work much on that end of the business."

"So you said." He had been upfront about that, at least. "What did you do? Before Gideon died, I mean."

"Public relations, mostly." He sat down on the edge of the desk, idly toying with a small stone paperweight that had been resting on its surface. "I soothed any water Gideon stirred up running the business."

"Did he do that often?"

His smile turned roguish. "All the time. He was good at coming up with new plans and inventions, and he was great at making sure he got what he needed to make them work, but he didn't pay much attention to the mess he left behind." The stone disappeared between his fingers, only to come back into view as he manipulated it with surprising ease. "Have you seen a picture of him yet?"

"No. Why?"

The stone between his fingers stilled as he reached to open one of the desk drawers. "Take a look."

He pulled out a framed photo and handed it to Cassie. The picture of the brothers had been taken at some sort of party, with people dancing and drinking in the background. David wore his usual grin, while Gideon looked more somber, but the two formed an obviously united front, each with an arm draped around his brother's shoulder.

"Twins?" she asked.

He nodded, but she hadn't needed his confirmation. The evidence was right before her eyes. At first, she had thought they were identical, but there were some noticeable differences. David's face was more open and enthusiastic, while Gideon's eyes had fine lines around them that lent him a harder edge. It made him look older than his brother. "Gideon was born first?"

"By five minutes. Sometimes I think I've spent my whole life trying to catch up to him."

"Did you ever resent him for that?"

"No." He met her gaze. "He was better at business than I am, better at inventing, too, but that didn't matter to me. He was my brother. He *is* my brother... even if he's not the person he used to be. I'd never do anything to harm him, no matter what people are saying. I didn't kill him."

"Say I believe you - which I'm not saying I do..."

"You can trust me, I swear. I'm sorry I didn't tell you the whole truth earlier, but I had to make sure you took Gideon's case. I had to know he was in good hands."

"Who else would have wanted him dead?"

"I don't know." The stone began to flash through his fingers again, picking up speed. "I've tried to figure it out, but I can't. Everyone loved him."

"What about love gone wrong? Any men or women who might have felt scorned?"

"Not that I know of. For the past few years, he's been completely focused on the family business. I don't think he had time to be involved with anyone."

"And you're sure the crash that killed him wasn't an accident?"

"I'm positive," David was quick to answer.

"Someone tampered with the electrical systems tied to the engine. Once they got hot enough, they shorted out, causing a fire and destroying his ability to control the car. There was no way he could have avoided the crash; we were just lucky no one else was injured."

"And you think that's why he's come back? To find whoever did this to him?"

"I don't know. I don't understand any of this. Why he was killed... why he came back... why he attacked those campers – if he did." Frustrated, he threw the stone back on the desk, watching its progress as it skimmed along the top and eventually made its way off the other side and onto the floor. "It doesn't make sense. Nothing makes sense anymore."

Seeing him so upset grieving his brother's death, Cassie felt a wave of sympathy. She knew what it was like to lose someone you loved; how desperate you became to retain any piece of the person you could.

She stepped towards him and placed her hand on his shoulder. "We'll find who did this to him, I promise. We'll give him what he needs to rest easy."

David looked up at her. "Thank you," he said, reaching out to cover her hand with his. "From both of us." The corners of his mouth edged up in a hesitant smile. "Gideon would have liked you, but that's not surprising. I can't imagine anyone not liking you."

His thumb brushed over the back of her wrist, and it sent a jolt of longing up her arm and through her body.

"Don't," she said, quickly pulling away from the

contact. "Just because I'm willing to give you the benefit of the doubt, it doesn't mean we're friends."

Tiny laugh lines appeared around his eyes as he asked, "Would it be so bad if we were?"

"Yes." *Maybe not to start, but eventually.* "I'm here for business only. Let's keep it that way."

Turning on her heel, she left the room before he had a chance to say something to change her mind.

Chapter Five

Cassie requested a copy of the mechanic's report from the crash to be sent to her, and then spent the morning investigating the household staff, questioning everyone from the head chef to the second assistant gardener, but no one gave her any clues about who would have wanted to kill Gideon, or what he might have come back for.

Maybe I'll have better luck with the scientists.

She was going to have to interview all of them – and soon – but for now, she had another avenue to pursue. She'd managed to schedule an appointment with Sasha Kramer, the survivor of the suspected zombie attack.

She checked her watch. The hospital was half an hour away; if she left now, she'd be early, but it's not like she was getting anything done here. Pulling out her cell phone, she called for a car and then headed down to the main foyer to wait for its arrival. As she waited by the door, a warm, deep voice came from behind her.

"Going somewhere?" The voice coursed through the air, sinking into her skin and creating a strong, steady buzz that had her nerves vibrating.

David.

Well, at least she didn't have to worry about her appearance. She was wearing a sand-colored dress with silver piping accentuating the bodice, and her hair was up in an elegant twist high on the back of her head, with one lock trailing free at her temple. The entire ensemble screamed, "competent professional."

Unfortunately, her hormones seemed to be screaming something entirely different.

She turned around, bracing herself to stay unaffected no matter what.

It was worse than she'd thought. He was dressed in a tailored navy suit, with his hair pulled back in the same style it had been when they'd first met. It made him look like sin made flesh, more tempting than any incubus she'd ever seen.

And more dangerous, too.

"I'm heading to the hospital to interview Sasha," she said, schooling her voice into professional disinterest. "I'm hoping she might have remembered more about who attacked her."

David paused, looking thoughtful. "That's a good idea," he said after a few seconds. "I'd like to come with you, if that's okay."

"It's not." The last thing she needed was to have him near. "I'm perfectly capable of handling it myself."

He smiled, and even though they were indoors, the air around them seemed to grow brighter. "I don't doubt it. I get the feeling there are very few things that phase you."

"Then why do I need you tagging along?"

His smiled faded, and the light faded back to normal.

"When I first hired you, you mentioned it might help to have someone who knows Gideon well working alongside you. And I've been visiting Sash since she was admitted," he said, his shoulders rising in a tense shrug. "We've become good friends. She might find it easier to talk to you if I'm there."

Damn. The woman had been through a terrifying ordeal... of course she would feel more comfortable with a familiar face present.

Normally Cass would have realized that right away, but there was something about this case that had her off-balance. She had to figure out what it was so she could stop it and get back to her usual self.

In the meantime, she had an apology to make.

"You're right, and I'm sorry. I shouldn't have snapped at you."

His shoulders loosened, returning to a more relaxed state. "Does that mean you'll let me come with you?" he asked, his eyes gleaming with an eager light.

"Don't get too excited," she growled, pushing down the traitorous pleasure spreading through her body. "You're still a suspect. I'm not about to let you say or do anything that might interfere with my investigation. You're going to have to follow my rules, which means you don't say a single word to Sasha without checking with me first."

"Whatever you want." His skin flushed, warming to a ruddy cinnamon. "Just tell me what you need, and I'll find a way to make it happen. I promise."

A car pulled up in the driveway before she could come up with a response that wouldn't get her in trouble. Luckily, the car in question was almost as attractive as his offer. A sweet little 1962 cherry-red Chevy convertible, it made her want to drool.

David sprang into action, rushing straight towards the driver's side door and holding it open for her. "I know it's a little old-fashioned," he said, "but it's the way my parents raised me. I hope you don't mind."

Cassie stalked around the car, ignoring the hand he was offering for assistance. She settled behind the wheel and breathed in the smell of worn leather and petroleum fumes.

Heaven on earth.

Busy savoring the intoxicating fragrance, Cassie was surprised when another scent joined the mix, as appealing – if not more – than that of the car. It reminded her of a late autumn day, with the cool, crisp air you get right before snow begins to fall. She turned her head to investigate its source.

David was standing next to her, the scent of his cologne wrapping around her and invading her senses. As he opened his mouth to speak, she revved the engine, drowning him out.

She didn't want to hear what he had to say.

He bent closer until his lips were practically grazing the outer shell of her ear. "The roads here are pretty quiet, so we can go as fast as you want." His voice washed over her like a caress, sending shivers down her spine. "Or as slow as you need. I'm happy with whatever pace you set."

The shivers doubled, and her hands clenched tightly around the steering wheel as he stood up and walked to the passenger's side. He settled into his seat, close enough that she could feel the heat rising from his body. It called out to her, begging her to draw closer and end the gap between them.

Slamming her foot on the gas pedal, she pulled out of the driveway, pushing the car as fast as she could.

Twenty minutes later, they arrived at the hospital.

Brightly lit with large windows and soothing pastel colors on the walls, the hospital had hanging ferns and potted Bonsai trees scattered around its hallways, disguising any smell of antiseptic and leaving a fresh, invigorating air in its place. The only thing that gave the building's real purpose away were the directional signs saying things like 'Reptilian/ Mammalian Hybrid Gastroenterology - third floor,' and 'Post-Transformative Cardiology – west wing.'

"Sasha's room is in the trauma center," David said, indicating the way. "It's right through this door."

Holding the door wide open, he waited for her to go first.

Several years ago, when the community had expressed a need for a post-Cataclysm medical center, the MacDuffs had stepped in. They'd bought the land needed and paid for the construction of a state-of-the-art hospital, with everything needed to treat a wide range of ailments ranging from broken arms (and legs, wings, and tentacles) to magical plagues. It was safe to say they had the most cutting-edge technology available.

It was equally safe to say the staff was aware one of their benefactors was on the premises. The employees were scurrying around like imps trying to impress their king. They pretended not to notice David was there, but she could see them sneaking glances when they thought he wasn't looking.

The cyclops stationed at the nurses' station wasn't as discrete. As he stepped up to her desk, she favored him with a slow, seductive fluttering of her eyelashes.

"David, it's been too long," she purred, standing up to greet him and revealing a uniform that displayed a level of cleavage Cassie suspected would be a health risk for cardiac patients. "What can I do for you?"

"Hi, Dana. We're here to see Sasha," David said, his gaze never straying from the nurse's face.

Dana smiled. "She's in x-ray, but she's due back any minute. I can keep you company till then." She walked around the desk and linked her arm through his.

He patted her hand affectionately before politely removing it from his arm.

"Thanks, D, but I think I'll be okay. We would like to speak to her doctor, if it's not any trouble."

"Anything for you," she simpered, shooting a look of pure adoration his way. "I'll have Dr. Bedard paged."

Dr. Bedard was Sasha's primary physician. She

had been involved in Sasha's care since she'd been brought to the hospital's emergency room and had been largely responsible for keeping the girl alive.

It didn't take long for the doctor to arrive. Her white jacket flapped briskly behind her as she walked towards them. As she got closer, Cassie noticed the heavy coating of downy fur covering her face and hands.

David performed the introductions then stepped back for Cassie to take the lead.

"Thank you for agreeing to see us, Doctor," she said.

"It's a pleasure to meet you. Diana told me you might be stopping by." The doctor shook Cassie's hand, careful to keep her claws from breaking Cassie's skin. "If you could come with me, please." She led them down the hallway and through a darkened doorway. Turning on the light, she explained, "We'll have more privacy here."

It was obviously an empty patient's room. It smelled vaguely of lemon-scented cleaning products and the sheets sported precise hospital corners.

"I take it you're here to question me about Ms. Kramer?"

"Yes. I'm hoping she'll be able to give us some clues as to what Gideon is up to."

"I thought as much. I'm afraid she doesn't remember much about the attack. It was a very disturbing incident for her, especially when combined with the death of her companion."

Cassie remembered David telling her the young

man had passed away before help had arrived. "We don't want to make things any more difficult for her than they already are, but we really do need to question her."

"I understand, but her health is my main priority. If you say or do anything to jeopardize it, I will end the interview immediately and have you escorted off the premises."

"I understand."

"Good." The doctor nodded in satisfaction, her claws retracting until they were barely visible. "Judging from what she does recollect," she continued, "and from the type and severity of the wounds she incurred, we believe it was someone with above normal strength. The average human wouldn't have been able to do so much damage – at least not by him or herself."

Cassie zeroed in on the last part of the statement.

"Can you be sure it wasn't more than one person?" Sentient zombies weren't big on working well with others. If there had been more than one attacker involved, it would indicate Gideon hadn't been involved.

"We can't be absolutely positive, but judging by the consistency of Sasha's injuries and from the statement she made to the police, it's a fairly safe assumption there was only one assailant."

Not good news.

There might not be concrete evidence Gideon had committed the attack, but someone who'd been a berserker before his death would have more than enough strength to inflict such vicious damage.

Cassie had wanted to dispatch Gideon as peacefully as possible, both for his sake and that of his family, but if he had already killed one person and hurt another, she might not have that choice. She'd have to stop him quickly, before he could injure anyone else.

Dr. Bedard shook her head, aware her audience had understood the significance of what she had told them. "I'm afraid there's not much more I can help you with. Sasha has been recovering quite well, perhaps she'll be able to tell you more. She should be returning to her room shortly. I'll let you know if she's feeling up to visitors."

As the doctor left, David sat down on the edge of the bed, his elbows on his knees and his head cradled in his steepled hands.

Cassie perched cautiously beside him, the mattress dipping slightly beneath her. She didn't want to look at him, didn't want to see the vulnerability she knew she'd find. She kept her face turned to the window instead. "I'm sorry. I know this is hard on you."

His voice was quiet, a pale imitation of its usual self. "I thought I was ready for the worst, but I'm not." She heard the rustle of his suit as he shifted. Out of the corner of her eye, she saw his shoulders slump in utter dejection.

Part of her wondered if this was a trick... a clever way to gain her sympathy. It wouldn't be the first time a suspect had tried to play her, and he had already proved he wasn't completely trustworthy. But somehow, it didn't seem to matter. Even knowing he might be playing her for a fool, she didn't want to see him in pain.

"No one's ever ready for it. No matter how much you try to prepare yourself, it's still going to hurt. It still feels like you'll never be happy again."

"Will I?" He turned towards her. "Will the pain ever stop?"

"Not really." It wasn't something she liked to admit, but even though he had lied to her, he deserved to know the truth about this. "There are going to be times when it hits you out of the blue... when it comes rushing back like it just happened."

His hand brushed against hers. "Who did you lose?"

She pulled away, rising abruptly from the bed. "That's not important." Walking to the window, she focused on the clouds outside, ignoring the water welling in her eyes. She heard the rustle of his suit as he came to stand behind her, but she refused to turn around.

His hands came to rest on her shoulders, the contact warm and comforting. "It's important to me."

Taking a deep breath, she blinked rapidly, banishing the tears threatening to overflow. "Don't worry about me. I haven't lost anyone or anything I couldn't live without."

"That doesn't mean it isn't hurting you." He tugged on one shoulder, urging her to turn around.

Schooling her face to conceal her emotions, she allowed him to guide her until they were face to face. "Even if it did," she said, meeting his gaze with now-dry eyes, "I wouldn't discuss it with you."

He flinched and dropped his hands away from her. "You're still mad at me."

"You're damn right I'm mad. You interfered with my case."

"Cass, I'm sorry." Wincing, he rubbed his forehead and temple with one hand, roughly scrubbing his skin as if he could erase the memory of his actions. "I didn't mean to keep anything from you. It's just when I saw in your office, all I could think about was that I needed you to help Gideon. I was stupid. I didn't think about what withholding that information might look like."

"I'll tell you what it looks like. It looks like I can't trust you."

He shook his head, denying the accusation. "If I could go back and do everything differently, I would. Since I can't do that, I'm going to do whatever it takes to prove I will never make that mistake again." He stared deeply into her eyes, dropping his voice to a low, intimate pitch. "I'll tell you anything you want to know. Just ask me, and I swear to you, I will give you nothing but the complete truth."

She stared into his eyes, trying to get an accurate read on him. He didn't shy away; his warm brown eyes locked onto hers, wide with what appeared to be sincerity and something else she couldn't identify.

She took a step closer. "I'll think about it. But you should know I don't give second chances often. And I never give third ones."

He leaned towards her until she could feel the heat from his body and the rising surge of her own hormones in response.

"You won't have to," he said, his voice quiet but determined. He inched closer, until the cloth of his suitcoat brushed lightly against the front of her dress, sending a shiver down her spine. "You can count on me."

God, she wanted to believe him...

Suddenly, a shrill repetitive beep pierced the air.

"What is that?" she asked, looking around to find the source of the disruption.

It was coming from an inner pocket of David's suit coat.

His eyes widened. "I had a security system installed in Sasha's room. She must have hit the panic button."

David bolted out of the room.

Cassie followed immediately after. By the time they reached Sasha's room, she had pulled up beside him. As she tried to go through the doorway in front of him, however, he stretched out an arm, blocking her from entering.

A group of workers bustled around a tiny figure lying still on the bed. Bandages covered most of the woman's face, but the little Cassie could see of it was alarmingly pale. Dr. Bedard was in the forefront, snapping out orders to nurses and technicians alike.

A tube leading to an intravenous bag was quickly attached to one of the figure's arms, and an oxygen mask placed over her nose and mouth.

"Sasha?" Cassie asked, even though she knew what the answer would be.

"Yes," David answered. He looked almost as pale as Sasha did, emotion bleaching his skin to a ghostly shadow of its normal appearance.

The doctor diligently continued her work until her patient began to stabilize. Eventually, the monitor next to her bed changed to a steady beat. No longer necessary, the technicians packed up their equipment.

As they wheeled the heavy machines out, Cassie slipped into the room.

She approached the bed, keeping her voice low enough not to disturb the sleeping girl. "What happened? Is she alright?"

"She is now, but it was close." Dr. Bedard gently lifted the edge of the bandage covering Sasha's throat, revealing two short thick bruises crossed over each other on the front, and four longer ones wrapped around each side, continuing towards the back of her neck.

There was no question in Cassie's mind what had made the marks. "Someone tried to strangle her."

"Yes." The doctor bared her canines in an angry snarl. "Fortunately, she managed to fight him off and hit the alarm."

David shook his head. "Who would do something like that?"

"I don't know why," she growled, "but we think

we know who. There was a witness who caught a brief look at him." Holding her arms rigidly at her sides as if she were trying to contain herself, the doctor's fingers spasmed, and Cassie watched as the other woman's claws extended to their full reach.

Cassie quickly moved forward, stepping between the doctor and David. "What did they see?" she asked, drawing the were's attention away from him. "Who did this?"

With her eyes looked onto Cassie, Dr. Bedard took several deep breaths, her chest heaving as she struggled to calm herself.

"It was a zombie," she said when she had finally collected herself sufficiently. She craned her neck to look past Cassie and towards where David stood, wide-eyed and disbelieving. "It had to have been Gideon."

***

The hospital's coffee was better than Cassie had expected – hell, it was probably the best coffee she'd ever had – but she could barely bring herself to drink it. Not when David was sitting across the table from her, looking as if he'd lost all the happiness he'd had left in the world. The deep brown of his eyes somehow seemed darker, as if sorrow had stolen their inner light and cast its shadow over them.

He had a coffee of his own, but she didn't think he'd taken a single sip. Instead, he'd kept it clenched in both hands, holding it so tightly she thought it might shatter.

"They said they didn't get a good look." His fingers flexed uneasily around the cup as he stared into it. "Just because it was a zombie, it doesn't mean it was Gideon."

"The odds are against it." She knew he was suffering, but she couldn't give him false hope. If she did, it would only hurt him more in the long run. "Very few people come back as zombies. The likelihood someone else reanimated and attacked Sasha is next to nothing."

He looked up, meeting her gaze. "A slim chance is still a chance. There's a possibility he's innocent." The words sounded confident, but she could hear the tremor underneath them. "Isn't there?"

She knew she should tell him no, but when she opened her mouth to do so, she found the words wouldn't come.

"Maybe," she found herself saying instead. "There's no way of knowing for sure until we find him, but I suppose it's not totally impossible."

His face lit up, and something in Cassie's heart lightened in response. Knowing he was feeling better - and that she had some small part of it - made her feel as if a flock of butterflies had set up residence inside her chest.

"So what do we do?" he asked, leaning eagerly towards her. "If it would help, I could have my assistant research whether or not there have been any reports of other zombies in the area."

"It couldn't hurt."

"I'll get him started on it right away."

"I also want to investigate the area where Sasha and her friend were camping."

"Not a problem. I'll take you to the camp site as soon as my meetings are finished. It shouldn't be long."

"That won't be necessary."

He looked questioningly at her.

"It's better if you're not involved with this any more than necessary. You said yourself; there are people who hold you responsible for Gideon's death." Until recently, she'd been one of them, but her doubts were beginning to melt faster than the wicked witch of the west at a water park. He *had* lied to her, but she didn't think he was lying about Gideon. He cared about his brother too much to have wanted to hurt him. "I don't want them thinking you're trying to influence the investigation."

"I suppose you're right, but you shouldn't go alone. It's not safe."

"I'll be fine. I'm used to these things; it's my job."

He set his cup on the table and reached out to cover one of her hands with his. "I know, but that doesn't mean you should take unnecessary risks." His thumb brushed over her skin, and it was all she could do not to lean into the touch. "Why don't you take Striker with you? He's familiar with the area, and it might help to have another set of eyes."

"I don't want to waste any more time." Her heart was beating an unsteady rhythm, and it was becoming harder to breathe normally. "Every minute I delay makes the trail colder."

"Then I'll give him a call and have him meet you there. Please," he begged, his fingers tightening gently around hers, "it will make me feel better knowing you have some backup."

She meant to pull her hand away- she swore that's what she'd been trying to do – but somehow, when she tried to move, their hands somehow joined together, their fingers intertwined.

"Alright." She stared down at the connection, unable to tear her eyes away. "If it'll make you happy, I suppose I could make an exception for you."

"It will."

He grinned, and the butterflies took flight, turning somersaults in her heart.

Chapter Six

The first zombies to show up after the Cataclysm were puppet zombies, controlled by people who had developed the ability to use wild magic. It took much longer for sentient zombies to appear.

***

Cassie strode down the dirt road leading to the campsite – a task significantly hindered by the fact that she was wearing four-inch open-toed sling backs. She should have changed into her four-inch hiking boots, but after what had happened back at the hospital, she'd realized she couldn't spend a second more on this job than she had to.

She should have pulled away the second David had taken her hand. She should have explained to him, calmly and rationally, that she was there strictly for business, and that even if she hadn't been, she still wouldn't be interested in someone like him.

So why hadn't she?

It had to be hormonal. It had been too long since her last relationship – disastrous as it had been – and her body was merely trying to make up for lost time.

That's all it was. She couldn't let that fool her into thinking it could be something more.

She'd rushed out of the hospital, desperate to get on with solving the case and getting away from him. Unfortunately, the site was at least a mile and a half away from the main house, accessible only by a narrow hiking trail, and it was giving her entirely too much time to think.

How the hell did I get into this mess?

She wasn't the type of woman to let herself get warm and fuzzy over a guy, and she wasn't the type to believe in happy endings. Her curse made it too dangerous.

*But what if there **is** a way to break the curse... something I haven't tried yet...*

She really should try to find out. Not because of David, of course. Just for future reference.

Pulling out her phone, she called Ash's number. It went straight to voicemail, so she launched directly to the point. "Ash, call me back as soon as you get this. Nothing life threatening, but I need your help. I'll be waiting to hear from you."

With that done, she clicked off the call and took a closer look at her surroundings. A dense thicket of trees bracketed the sides of the path, forming a pleasant corridor of shade. About fifty yards ahead, the dirt on the road had been replaced by gravel leading to a ring of stone that encircled a man-made encampment.

She'd reached the site where Sasha had been staying.

What was left of it, anyway.

Striker hadn't arrived at the site yet, but Cassie decided not to wait for him. He could catch up when he got there.

Examining the encampment, she was impressed by the damage that had been done. The police report had told her what to expect but seeing it first-hand was altogether more compelling. The tent was barely standing - one wall had been sliced from top to bottom, leaving a gaping hole with its edges stirring in the breeze. In the clearing itself, she could see long grooves etched into the dirt, showing where a body had been dragged. Large uneven patches of ground were stained a deep rust color, and the metal grating from the fire pit had been thrown a considerable distance across the campsite.

She examined the slash marks on the tent.

He attacked here first.

Two precise cuts. Most likely, the zombie had taken a knife and deliberately slit the thin fabric, allowing him to sneak in silently to where Sasha's companion had been sleeping. Caught unaware, there would have been no chance for him to escape.

The drag marks on the ground went from the tent to the fire in an uninterrupted straight line; the man must have been dead by then or he would have struggled. Deeper indentations indicated where the zombie had crouched down beside the body. That would be consistent with what the reports said the attacker had been doing when Sasha had returned from her walk.

Apparently, Sasha had seen the zombie from behind, and assumed her boyfriend had woken up from his nap and come out of the tent to tend the fire. She'd said she'd called out to him, letting him know she was back.

She'd also said everything after that was blurry. All she could remember was that her attacker's skin had been pale, his flesh cold and clammy as he struck at her over and over again. She'd been sure he was going to kill her, but for some reason, he'd stopped suddenly and walked away, leaving her for dead.

But why had he stopped? Why had he dragged Sasha's boyfriend out to the fire in the first place? Had he been looking for something? And why had he thrown the grate away from the fire? The zombie had to have been the one to do it; no one else would have been able to touch the heated metal with their bare hands.

Unless their hands weren't bare...

Cassie crossed to the grate. There were tiny bits of cooked flesh adhered to it.

She pried a piece off with one of the knives she had brought with her and dropped it into a sterilized Ziploc, putting the whole thing back into her oversized shoulder bag to have it tested later. She found other inconsistencies scattered around the grounds, and she collected those, too, meticulously cataloging them.

Satisfied she had found all she was going to, she started back down to the castle. She was halfway down the path when she ran into Striker coming from the other direction.

With the sun behind him, he seemed to be outlined in an unearthly glow. The light outlined his body and hair, creating a golden corona around him. She had to admit, it was an appealing sight. He was exactly the type she normally went for, but the butterflies in her chest stayed still when she was with him.

Luckily, judging by the sullen expression on his face, he seemed to have gotten over his initial attraction to her. He seemed more annoyed with her than anything.

"Dave sent me to examine the site with you," he snapped. "Told me you were tinkering around up there trying to figure out if Gideon really attacked those people and said you could use some help."

"Already been and finished. No help necessary..." She held her arms out to the side to show him she was okay. "And look, I didn't even break a nail..."

Striker's eyes narrowed, a sardonic edge to their bottle-green depths. He scanned her from head to toe. "Looks good to me," he growled. "I told him he was worrying for nothing. Looks like I wasted my time heading out here."

Turning abruptly, he started to make his way down the path and back to the house. "Come on," he said, looking back over his shoulder, "I'm sure you're anxious to get back to the house and continue your vacation."

Excuse me?! Vacation?

Cassie ran after him.

"Hold on." When he didn't slow, she pulled at his arm, forcing him to stop. "Do you have a problem with how I'm doing my job?"

He erupted into harsh laughter. "Are you doing it?" A cold light came into his eyes as he stared down at her. "It didn't take you long to search the place. You couldn't have looked very hard."

"I did what I needed to do." Admitedly, the site hadn't revealed much, but even the smallest of clues could lead to something bigger.

Striker didn't seem to agree. "Shouldn't you be less worried about why Gideon went after a couple of dumb bystanders and more concerned with how he got killed?" he scowled, crossing his arms over his chest in an obvious challenge.

Unintimidated by the display, Cassie issued a challenge of her own. "Are you so sure it was Gideon who did it?"

He drew back with a visible start. "Who else would it be?"

Suddenly, the sound of a twig snapping came from the side of the road.

Cassie drew one of the heavier knives out from her bag as more rustling came from among the trees. "What was that?"

Striker moved to one side of the area the sound had come from. He motioned for her to position herself a few feet away before calling out, "You might as well show yourself. We know you're there."

Silence greeted them. Apparently, whoever was out there wasn't in the mood to introduce themselves.

"Could it have been the dryad, Nim?" Cassie whispered.

"Not likely." Striker moved further into the trees, checking the sightlines for any sign of the intruder. "She sticks to her forest, doesn't come up this far."

"Then it's probably nothing." There was no doubt in Cass's mind someone was out there. When the rustling they had heard earlier had stopped; so had every other noise. There were no birds calling, no insects chirruping. Something was disturbing their territory.

She backed away, never taking her eyes off of the woods. The forest was a bad place to fight. Better to pretend they were retreating in order to lure the intruder out into the open. "Let's just head back."

Unfortunately, Striker didn't have the same idea. He forged deeper into the brush. She rapidly lost sight of him and was just about to go in after him when he burst through the trees, running onto the path.

His chest was heaving and his face was flushed red. "Get back to the house, now!" he screamed, pulling a heavy duty Hi-Point 9MM from his jacket. "I'll hold them off the best I can."

Behind him, a pack of zombies crashed into sight.

Oh, fuck

The zombies lurched out of the forest. Two men, one woman... and all in the final stages of decomposition. There wasn't a single strand of hair -

or a complete set of limbs - amongst the three.

"Run!" Striker screamed again, lifting his gun to take aim at the zombie at the front of the pack. "I'll draw them away."

His gun erupted several times, shooting holes into the bodies of all three undead.

It didn't slow them down. It didn't even catch their attention. Contrary to popular belief, guns were almost useless against zombies, even if you were good enough to guarantee a headshot.

The zombies continued on their path towards Cassie.

Striker began to flail his arms. "Over here, moldy," he yelled.

The female paused, looking confused.

"What are you doing?! Run!" Striker's movements became more erratic as he tried to draw the other undeads' attention, as well, but they continued to shamble after Cassie.

Time to get to work.

Reaching into her bag, she dropped the knife before pulling out a color-coordinated high-voltage cattle prod and machete set and smiling at the zombies.

"I'm going to give you one chance," she said, keeping her words slow and distinct enough that they might be able to hear her even with their distinct lack of ears. "Stop where you are, and my friend over here and I will dig you some nice, comfy graves to settle down in. Or," she continued, dropping into fencing form and activating the prod, "I can use this."

The zombies kept going, marching towards her with a mindless determination.

"No!" Striker screamed, waving his arms even more frantically. "We can't reason with them. We need to attack."

"We need to take them out, but there's no need to be cruel about it. They were human once. Bits of them still might be."

"They're mindless animals. It's kill or be killed!" Bringing up his gun up, he fired several more bullets. One of the shots clipped the female zombie in the chin, and fragments of its jaw went flying to the ground.

The undead's eyes went wide a look of dimly remembered horror, and it began to tremble.

Oh shit.

Feral zombies were always dangerous, but if you knew what you were doing, it wasn't difficult to contain them. For the most part, their attacks were slow and uncoordinated, and their hearts – if they had hearts left – never seemed to be in the fight unless you woke up the instinct for survival that had turned them into a zombie in the first place.

And apparently, the zombie Striker had hit had just enough instinct left to turn it into a dangerous killing machine.

Knowing there wasn't much time before the zombie succumbed to a mindless bloodlust, Cassie leaped forward, jolting the first of the undead males with the cattle prod. It fell to the ground, collapsing in an ungainly heap. Seeing a helpless supply of meat located so nearby, its companion changed directions and stooped down for a midday snack.

Unfortunately, in the time it took to take them down, the female had grown increasingly agitated. Its one remaining hand had come up to cradle its face, and its eyes locked on Striker, targeting him as the focus of all of its confused misery and pain.

No time for niceties.

Tightening her grip on the machete, Cassie lopped off the head of the zombie dining on its compatriot. Within seconds, another quick flick of her wrist decapitated the one who had served as lunch, sending it, too, to a quick, if messy, peace.

Rising quickly, Cassie trained her sights on the remaining zombie.

Its trembling had gotten stronger, growing until its whole body was shaking violently. With an agonized roar, it lurched towards Striker.

Shit. Too late.

A few seconds faster and Cassie could have ended this painlessly.

With a resigned sigh, she dropped the cattle prod she'd been holding in her left hand and reached into the bag for her flamethrower.

Striker was standing immobilized as the zombie stalked towards him, picking up speed and drawing dangerously close. As it came within striking distance, he finally seemed to realize the danger he was in. He shot at the zombie, empty clicks sounding as his finger continued to tighten on the trigger even after he was out of ammunition. She could see the panic enter his eyes as he dropped the gun and turned to run.

It was the worst thing he could have done.

Cassie knew there wasn't any time to lose. Striker was too close to the zombie for Cassie to use the flamethrower, and at this distance, she couldn't get a good enough angle with the machete to take the zombie's head off, but there were other options…

Her right hand flexed on the grip of the machete, and she visualized the path she'd need it to take. After the split second it took to cement the trajectory in her mind, she lifted her arm and threw the deadly weapon.

It tumbled end over end until it reached its destination, its handle striking Striker in the temple and knocking him unconscious.

She felt a moment of guilt for the headache he was probably going to wake up with, but it was for his own good. Running would only have made the zombie chase him harder.

Deprived of the thrill of a chase, the zombie stopped and looked for the source of the projectile.

"Yeah," Cassie said, politely waving the hand holding the flamethrower. "That would be me."

The zombie leapt for Cassie's throat.

Cass dove to the side, dodging the attack and rolling back to her feet before flicking the torch's ignition switch.

Nothing.

She tried it again.

Shit.

She could hear the hiss of the gas, but it wasn't catching fire.

The zombie screamed - well, as much as it was able to with half of its jaw missing - and lurched towards her, its arm extended and fingers curled into a grasping claw.

It was moving faster now, adrenalin fueling its rage.

Cassie ducked under its arm and then spun around to face it, putting herself between it and the unconscious Striker. "I know we've just met, but you seem like a lovely person. Why don't we forget about this whole mess? Maybe go out for a coffee?"

The zombie's lifeless blue eyes narrowed in anger. "Kill you…"

"Okay, so I guess you're more of a tea person. I can work with that." She flicked the switch again, hoping for a different result, but it still wasn't working.

Why the hell was wrong with it? Was it clogged?

The machete was somewhere on the ground behind her, lying where it had fallen after hitting Striker. She could probably get to it before the zombie got to her, but if she didn't make it in time, she would be putting him at risk.

She took a step forward, moving towards her opponent and away from Striker. "How do you feel about chai?"

The zombie shivered violently, then bared jagged and decayed teeth in a twisted snarl. "You die now."

As it threw itself towards her in a headlong charge and knocked her to the ground, Cassie's hand slipped over the handle of the flamethrower, catching on a small piece of metal on the side.

Oh, that's right. I had a safety switch put in after the Toledo incident.

The zombie's fingers wrapped around her throat, cutting off her air, and its dirt-encrusted fingernails dug into her flesh, threatening to pierce the skin. Bringing her knees up to her chest, Cassie planted the flat part of her shoes against the zombie's chest. As she kicked it back towards the tree line, her thumb shoved the safety latch to the "off" position.

A spark leapt out of the flamethrower's nozzle, igniting a column of fire.

That's more like it.

"Now," Cass said, getting to her feet and brandishing the weapon in front of her, "are you sure you don't want to change your mind about that chai?"

The zombie hesitated, and for a second Cassie thought she was getting through to it, but the moment was short-lived. Striker shifted, mumbling something in his delirium, and his incoherent mumblings were enough to set it off again. With eyes filled with more hatred than an undead should be capable of, it made one final charge towards Cassie.

She brought the flamethrower up before it could even get close.

It caught fire instantly, desiccated flesh and decaying cloth catching ablaze with equal alacrity.

Chapter Seven

Cassie made her way back to the house carrying the still-unconscious Striker in a fireman's hold, his head banging into her ass with every step she took. With one arm wrapped around the back of his knees, she shifted him to rest more securely on her shoulder.

He meant well, she'd give him that. He just wasn't any good at dealing with the undead. Most people weren't. That's why they needed someone like her.

It was also why she was going to have to come up with a polite way to tell her employers she had knocked their head of security into a semi-catatonic state.

Hopefully they won't be so mad that they fire me immediately.

She had saved his life. That should count for something, shouldn't it? And if it didn't, maybe her news about Gideon would.

***

It counted for something. In fact, it counted for a whole lot of something.

The MacDuffs had been nothing but gracious about the whole incident. In fact, they were so happy to have Striker back unharmed - or at least relatively so - that Cassie was now the proud recipient of a substantial monetary bonus and a case of some of the finest single-malt scotch known to man or myth.

Leaning back into the plush upholstery of the sitting-room chair, she took a long sip of the self-same scotch and savored the prospect of telling David his brother might not have been behind Sasha's attack after all. It wasn't often she got to give her clients good news. Usually she was the one letting them know their loved ones were gone forever. It felt nice to give someone a reason for hope.

It felt even better that the someone was David. She could picture his smile when he found out. She couldn't wait to see it.

As if the universe had heard her unspoken wish, he strode in through the doorway.

"Cassie!" He was stalking towards her, his face clouded by worry and anger. "They told me what happened." Before she knew what was happening, he had wrapped his arms around her and enfolded her into his embrace. "Thank God you're okay."

Better than okay. Telling herself a few stolen moments of indulgence wouldn't be that dangerous, she took a deep breath and drew the clean, revitalizing scent of his cologne deep into her system. "It was no big deal. There were only three of them. I've handled a lot more than that."

A shudder coursed through his body, causing a

tremor under her cheek. "How many more? And how often?"

She wasn't normally one to brag, but since he had asked...

"Anything less than a dozen doesn't even count as breaking a sweat." She smiled proudly. "But not all that often. Once, maybe twice a week, tops."

His grasp tightened, startling her. "Not alone, though, right?" His voice deepened to a husky growl. "Tell me you don't try to take on that many by yourself."

Lifting her head, Cassie stared up into a face that looked anything but pleased by her accomplishments.

What the hell?

"There's no *trying* involved," she said, hackles rising as he continued to scowl. "It's my job, and I do it damn well. Do you have a problem with that?"

David nodded. "Yes, I do. I have a problem with you being reckless."

She pushed away from him. "I'm not reckless."

"Really?" His head cocked to the side and his eyebrows raised in disbelief. "You could have fooled me. You went to the site of a possible zombie attack by yourself when you could have had backup if you'd just waited for Striker... like you promised you would!"

"It's not my fault he took so long to get there." Striker's words from earlier echoed in her thoughts, and she found herself hurling his accusation back at David. "Did you expect me to longue around the house like I'm on vacation? I'm not a damsel in distress, and

I don't need a bodyguard to protect me."

He let out a heavy sigh. "I'm not saying you need protection, but you shouldn't be doing this alone. You were the one who told me you usually work with a team."

Oh really... he wants to go there?

"And whose fault is it they aren't here?"

He winced, rubbing at his temple. "That may not have been one of my better ideas." One edge of his mouth quirked up in a rueful smile. "In my defense, back at your office, I couldn't imagine needing to hire anyone but you. You are pretty impressive."

"Damn right I am. So why do you think I need help now? What's changed?"

"What's changed," he said, staring at her with an odd expression in his deep brown eyes, "is that the more I get to know you, the less I can stand the thought of something happening to you." His hand came up to caress her cheek, the warmth of his palm sinking into her skin and setting her on fire. "You may be the best there is..."

"Not *may* be. I am."

"... but that doesn't mean you're invincible." He stepped closer, until there was only a hair's breadth between them. "And I don't want to lose you."

Shock stole her breath, leaving her dizzy and strangely uncertain. Leaning into his touch to steady herself, her fingers brushed against the front of shirt. "Nothing happened," she said, not understanding why it mattered so much to him but wanting to reassure him, nonetheless. "I didn't get hurt."

His free hand rose to her hip. "This time. But what about next time?" His fingers clenched with an almost desperate urgency.

"David…"

Looking as if he wanted to devour her, his head dipped towards her. Tugging on his shirt, she yanked him the rest of the way. She wanted to taste him everywhere, to feel the texture of his skin on her tongue and his heat under her hands. She bit his lower lip, nipping it softly and reveling in the growl that rose from him in reaction.

His fingers grazed her collarbone, skimming over it with a touch so light and reverent it made her legs unsteady. If he hadn't been holding her up, she would have collapsed to the floor in a boneless puddle.

God, what was happening to her? She was used to lust, but this was something more… something new. It felt like a promise.

Things like this didn't happen to her.

They couldn't.

She broke the kiss, shoving him away before she could do more damage.

David was the first to break the resulting silence. "Cassie, I'm sorry." He was looking at her like he was the one who had screwed up… like he was the one who had ruined everything. "I shouldn't have presumed…"

"No, it's not that." She couldn't let him think it was his fault, but what was she supposed to tell him? "It's me… I just…"

Suddenly, her phone began to buzz. Bark at the

Moon by Ozzy Osbourne sang through the speaker, filling the room with its insistent chorus. Cassie had never thought of herself as a coward, but in that moment, she'd gladly accept the title. "I just have to answer my phone. I've been waiting for this call. It's, uh, very important. And private."

"Oh. Of course. I don't want to interfere with your work." One corner of his mouth quirked up in a lopsided grin. "I think I've already messed up enough for one day." He paused, gazing at the floor before looking up to meet her eyes. "But maybe I could see you later... if it's alright with you..."

Cass stared at him. "Uh, sure," she stammered. "That would be nice."

"Good. I'll be looking forward to it." He turned and left the room.

She watched him go, torn between the desire to chase after him and the desire to chase him away before things got worse. Luckily, the ringing of her phone called her back to reality before she could do anything stupid. She slid her finger over the phone's screen to accept the call.

"Cass here. What's up, Ash?"

"I was about to ask you the same thing. I got your message - what's so urgent?" As she spoke, explosions underscored with unearthly screams sounded in the background.

"Is that live gunfire, or are you playing Call to Arms 16 again?" At Casa Pendleworth-Miller, it could be either. Like most weres', Ash lived with an extended clan. In her case, that meant herself, her parents, two older sisters, a younger brother, assorted aunts and uncles and their children, and an over-sized griffin who thought he was a lap dog.

The griffin was the sanest of the bunch.

"A little of both," Ash admitted, a spate of gunfire reverberating through the connection. "Josh and I rigged some virtual reality goggles to our shooting range. We're doing some awesome new practice runs."

Josh was Ash's brother. When Cassie had first met him, he had been nothing but a scrawny techno-geek, but in the last few years, he had begun to follow in his father's paw prints. Now he was a techno-geek with rock-hard abs and a lethal uppercut.

"How's the little runt doing? Tell him I said hi."

"I will... now quit stalling. What's wrong?"

Cassie should have known better than to think she could get away with concealing the truth. The two women had been friends for too long.

"You remember what I told you about my client?"

"You mean the Scottish lord you absolutely, definitely weren't interested in?"

Cass could practically feel her friend's smugness oozing through the phone's receiver. She had half a mind to hang up on her, but the saner half knew Ash would be laughing too hard to call back right away, and she needed help immediately. "That's the one."

"Tell me everything."

"I kissed him," she blurted out, blushing as

she remembered how she'd clung to him, holding on when she should have been pushing him away. "I didn't mean to. I... kind of forgot about my curse. Well, not so much forgot about it as completely ignored it."

Ash whistled. "That must have been one hell of a kiss."

"You have no idea." Her cheeks grew warmer, turning bright red. "But it's not just the way he kisses. Something happens to me whenever he's around."

"Something good?"

"Something great. He makes me feel like I have a shot at something real."

When it finally came, Ash's reply normal exuberance was toned down to a quiet sincerity. "You know I've always thought you pay too much attention to that stupid curse."

"I have to." Cassie's stomach flipped over as she thought about the damage she'd done to other men. "I don't want to be responsible for ruining anyone else's life."

Ash sighed. "What do you want me to do?

Cassie had thought about it, and as far as she could tell, there was only one option. "I haven't had any luck breaking the curse, but maybe if I could find the woman who cast it and explain I didn't know Drew was seeing her, too, that he'd told me I was the only one...maybe she'd remove it."

"Didn't you try explaining that when it happened?"

"Yes, but she was upset at the time." It wasn't

easy finding out the guy who supposedly loved you was cheating on you with another woman.

"You were upset, too," Ash said, "But you didn't cast any spells on her."

"It wasn't her fault he was lying to us both."

"It wasn't yours, either."

"Ash…" Cassie warned, not wanting to get into an argument they'd had too many times before. "Drop it."

"Fine," the other woman grudgingly relented. "I'll try and track her down for you. I'll even ask Mom to help."

"Do you think she will?" If anyone could find a way to locate the missing wizard, it would be Miranda Pendleworth. Not only was she a kitsune and a sorceress, she had all the additional resourcefulness that came with being a mother.

"You know she will. She thinks of you like a daughter." A particularly loud explosion came from Ash's end of the phone. "Shoot… Josh got to the final battle. I can't let him beat it without me - he'd never let me hear the end of it. Was there anything else you needed?"

"Not that I can think of."

"Okay then, I'll let you know as soon as I have any news. Talk to you later." The call disconnected abruptly.

Cassie put the phone in her pocket. She felt lighter, as if someone had opened a window and let in the first breath of spring. A sense of revitalization swept through her, airing out the closed-up corners of her soul and chasing the gloom away.

With both Ash and her mom on the job, it was only a matter of time before they found the wizard, and Cassie would finally have a chance to apologize properly. To make amends, and maybe, just maybe, to finally have a relationship with a man she could trust.

Not that she had anyone in particular in mind, of course. Just… theoretically.

Finding the curse-caster was the key to it all, and it was going to be all Cassie could do to contain herself until Ash called with the news that the search had been successful.

Oh shit… news… I forgot to tell David about the zombies I fought earlier, and about what they might mean.

In their argument and the resulting aftereffects, she'd gotten distracted. And who wouldn't have been, she reasoned, remembering the warmth of his hand on the small of her back and the heat that had spread everywhere else as his tongue stroked the roof of her mouth…

Maybe I should go look for him… after all, it wouldn't be right to keep him in the dark longer than necessary.

She set out with a spring in her step.

Fifteen minutes later, she still hadn't found him. She'd looked everywhere on the first floor and he was nowhere to be found. The sun had already set, and it was almost time for dinner.

I suppose I could wait till then. I could use a change of clothes, anyway. The dress she was wearing still had lightly toasted zombie bits covering it.

She was just heading back downstairs after freshening up when she saw Malcolm MacDuff coming up the other way to meet her.

"Ah, hello dear," he said, rushing up the steps. "How are you feeling? No lasting effects from your heroic actions, I hope? You should be taking it easy to make sure. Perhaps you'd like to take a nap before dinner? We can have the cook push back the time... or I can have him prepare a tray for you if you don't feel up to a big meal. Something light... a nice bowl of broth and a big glass of whiskey will set you to rights... or maybe something heartier to build your strength back up... We could make a lasagna and open up a bottle of Barolo wine."

Cassie couldn't help but smile. "I'm fine, thank you. No need to change anything for me; I'm looking forward to dinner with the family. I was actually hoping to speak to David before then. I don't suppose you've seen him lately, have you?"

"I think I caught a glimpse of him a few minutes ago. It looked like he was headed for the library."

"Thank you."

"Don't mention it, my dear." He took her hand and raised it to his lips, brushing it with the same kind of gentle kiss she had seen David give to the wood nymph. "It was my pleasure."

Before she could say another word, he scurried away.

Turning around to make her way back up to the second floor, she found her way to the library. The thick wooden door was closed, but she could see light seeping from underneath it.

She knocked lightly. "David?"

There was no answer, so she tried again, rapping harder. There was still no reply, so she turned the handle and inched the door open. "David? Are you in here?"

The room was empty, but it looked like someone had been there recently. A small light on a side table had been turned on, and one of the windows had been opened to let in fresh air.

A gentle breeze swept in, stirring a pile of papers scattered across the top of the desk.

Cassie walked over to examine the pile. It was the summary of the car crash from the mechanic. David must have seen it when it was delivered and brought it up here for her to look at.

He was so thoughtful.

A creak came from beside her, and Cassie turned to see a door – cleverly designed to blend in with the library's décor and almost impossible to spot if you didn't know it was there - swing open.

Of course there are secret corridors. Why would anyone want a castle without them?

Partially hidden by the now-open door, she watched David move towards the desk. He stared down at the pile of papers, his spine bowed and his shoulders slumped.

I'd be depressed if I had to deal with that much paperwork, too.

Well, she could think of one way to cheer him

up...

"If that passage goes by my bedroom," she said, the corners of her mouth curling up in an unabashed grin, "I'm going to be really pissed you didn't stop in to say hi."

David's head jerked at the sound of her voice, and he turned to face her fully. As his eyes focused on hers, she realized her mistake.

Not David...

Gideon.

Even before death, there had been differences between the two brothers, but now those differences were magnified tenfold. They shared the same strong features, but Gideon's were twisted by desperation. His eyes were bloodshot, and his skin, while not bearing any signs of physical deterioration, had turned a pale and pasty white.

Not fully lost, but not far from it, either.

She could see it in the way he stood. His body had stiffened, his fists clenched so tightly that droplets of red fell from his palms onto the carpet below.

His body began to shake violently, and she knew she only had one chance. "Gideon, you don't want to do this. I know you didn't attack Sasha. Your family knows, too. They want to help you."

His shaking grew stronger, and Cassie's stomach lurched. She'd made matters worse.

"I don't want their help," he growled, his voice as dry and unwelcoming as a grave. "Tell them to stay the hell away from me."

"I'll give them the message, but I don't think they'll listen. They love you." If she could just keep him talking, maybe she could get through to him. "We can end this peacefully."

"Just stay out of this!" The black of his pupils expanded, obliterating all traces of brown as his berserker nature rose to the surface. Moving quickly, he snatched the papers off the desk and strode to the open window. "Before someone gets hurt."

"Gideon, wait!"

Too late. He was gone, throwing his legs over the sill and jumping down faster than she could reach him. He was on his feet in seconds, springing up and into a sprint.

At the rate he was going, she was going to lose him fast.

Cursing to herself, she climbed out onto the sill. The drop was only a few feet, but the ground below was pure gravel.

Shit. This is going to be murder on my heels.

She dropped to the ground, anyway.

Hoping she could catch him before he made it to the woods, she sprinted after him.

Chapter Eight

Even after the Cataclysm, some things didn't change. For example, all was still fair in love and war.

***

The branches overhead blocked out any light the moon might have cast, making Cassie's search almost impossible. Noise came from all directions, the sound of leaves rustling in the wind and animals scurrying around effectively camouflaging any hint of the direction Gideon had taken.

Roots twisted under Cassie's feet, tripping her up and slowing her down. She wasn't going to find him like this.

She spotted a movement in her peripheral vision, but it was only a badger annoyed by someone daring to trespass in its territory.

"Gideon! Come out, I just want to talk."

Nothing. Not that she expected an answer. It couldn't be that easy.

It was never that easy.

"Come on, Gideon. You came back to the house.

You obviously wanted something. If you tell me what it is, I can help you get it." *You can't hide forever.* She could hear footsteps, the heavy tread of a human as opposed to the lighter step of a forest dweller.

There.

She turned in the direction she thought it was coming from and moved cautiously forward. "I don't want to hurt you, Gideon. Your family hired me to make sure you get your peace." She pushed the limb of a hawthorn tree out of her way, hoping to get a better look, but it snapped back, hitting her in the face and obscuring her view again. "Shit."

She'd lost the trail again. He was gone, and there was no way to tell which way he went. She'd have to come out first thing in the morning when there was more light.

She looked for the path that had brought her into the forest, but it was gone, too. She wasn't sure which way took her back to the castle and which led further into the heart of the woods. She couldn't see the stars well enough to gauge her position, and the forest itself seemed to be shifting around her, disorienting her.

It had to be the dryad. She obviously didn't want anyone wandering around in her domain. Cass respected that, but she had a job to do.

"Knock it off, Nim," she yelled. "The sooner I get out of your woods, the sooner I can get my job done and quit disturbing you. You'll have your forest all to yourself."

Tree limbs extended towards Cassie, reaching

out to catch at her hair.

"I'm beginning to think this is personal." She couldn't possibly be jealous over David, could she? I mean, how would the nymph even know Cassie had kissed him?

No, it has to be something else.

"Look, Nim, I'm sorry for whatever I've done to make you mad, but we can work this out."

The only answer was a sharp tug, strong enough to make her eyes water.

"This is ridiculous," Cassie yelled, trying to free her hair from the tree's painful grasp. "We're strong, independent women with no reason to fight over a man. And with that being said, if you don't let me go right now, I'm going to get my flamethrower out."

The branches receded, releasing her from their grip.

"Thank you." Determined to be gracious in victory, she tried to filter most of the sarcasm from her voice. "Now how 'bout a path out of here?"

The woods remained still.

"Not gonna make it easy for me, huh?" Cassie complained. "Fine, I'll do it myself."

She began to pick her way out of the forest. She thought she was making progress when a sound from behind caught her attention.

Something was following her, moving rapidly and making an awful lot of noise. Maybe the dryad was sending one of the animals that lived in the forest after Cassie.

Whatever it was, it sounded big. She knew she

should have grabbed a weapon before chasing after Gideon, but there hadn't been time. She would just have to deal with whatever was coming after her.

At least I've got my shoes.

Sure, they were sexy as hell and made her legs look phenomenal, but that wasn't the reason Cassie wore four-inch heels. *Okay, maybe it was* one *of the reasons - but it wasn't the only one.* Her heels could inflict major damage in a fight.

There had been many times that a properly aimed kick from her stilettos had saved her life.

Cassie turned to face whatever was heading towards her. The sound of dead branches being crushed underfoot grew louder, mingling with a labored breathing. Trees parted, making way as the thing following her stepped into view.

Shadows clung to him, and his dark hair hung loose, falling to his shoulders and hiding some of his face, but she could still see enough to recognize the bloodless skin and fathomless black eyes.

Gideon.

Gideon moved towards her, and for the first time, she noticed the sword he was carrying. A lethal slash of finely honed Damascus steel, he held it as if it were an extension of his arm, part of his very being.

Where the hell had he gotten that?

"Stay back." She inched around until she had maneuvered into a position directly opposite of him. "There's no need for anything rash. I told you before, I'm not going to hurt you."

Not unless he made her, anyway.

She kept her voice calm and measured. "I know you're confused, Gideon, but I need you to put down the sword before this goes someplace neither of us wants it to go."

A flicker of confusion passed over his features, and he shook his head roughly.

"Cassie, it's me. It's David." He took a step forward, moving towards her with sword in hand. "Thank God you're here. I was worried something had happened to you."

"Stop." She took a cautious step backwards, maintaining her original distance.

The zombie raised his hands in a gesture of surrender, but Cassie noticed he didn't let go of his weapon.

"Just give me a second and I'll clear everything up," he said, never taking his eyes off Cassie or raising his voice. "Nim," he yelled, "cut it out."

The forest swiftly retreated, leaving them standing in a circular clearing. As the crescent moon shone high above, casting its glow down upon them, Cassie could see him more clearly. His flesh, which had appeared pale and bloodless in the dark shadows of the forest, revealed itself to be flushed with a ruddy glow, and his eyes, while darker than usual, held a lingering fear.

Shit. If she kept making stupid mistakes like that, David was going to think she didn't know what she was doing. "Sorry about that. I guess you two look more alike than I'd realized. So... what's up with the sword?"

He glanced at the weapon as if surprised he was holding it. "Nim told me someone's been crashing around in her forest, causing a lot of damage. I thought I'd check it out and see if I could do anything to help. I was heading back home when I heard you yelling." His fingers tightened around the hilt of the sword. "I thought you were in trouble."

Cassie grinned. It was sweet of him to worry, even if he hadn't needed to. "Only if you count getting lost like the proverbial babe in the woods trouble."

His grasp on the sword loosened. "I'm beginning to think you can find trouble anywhere," he replied, smiling to take the sting out of his words, "but I'm glad you're okay. I'm not sure how much help I would have been, anyway. I've never...." Whatever he had been about to say was lost as he saw the scratches on her face. "You're bleeding." In the space of a heartbeat, his face transformed. Anger turned him into the mirror image of his brother's photo, harder and more ruthless. "You need to go to the doctor."

"It's nothing, although I wouldn't mind showing your resident wood nymph how well I can handle a hatchet."

His body stiffened. "Nim did this? She hurt you?"

"Not intentionally." Cassie might have a debt to settle with the dryad, but she'd see to it herself. "I guess I wasn't paying enough attention to where I was going, and I ran into one of her trees."

Some of the tension drained from his shoulders. "I'm still taking you out of here." He moved closer, reaching for her elbow in an attempt to guide her. "You need to have those looked at."

"I told you, it's nothing." She didn't know why he was getting so upset. She had survived far worse than this.

"It's not nothing." He took a deep breath. "God, woman, why are you being so stubborn?" With an exasperated sigh, he reached into his pocket and pulled out a neatly folded white handkerchief. "If you won't go to the doctor, then at least stand still while I make sure the scratches don't get infected."

He began to move the cloth over her cheek in soft sweeping circles, wiping away the blood. "I know you think I worry too much, but I can't help it. I'm protective of the people I care about." He was excruciatingly gentle, but the light touch was enough to send shivers coursing down Cassie's spine. He finished cleaning the blood off, but his hand remained on her cheek, stroking it with a light brush. "And I've come to care about you." The handkerchief fluttered to the ground as he shifted his hand to tuck an errant piece of hair behind her ear. "More than I probably should."

"Oh." Cassie stared at him, mesmerized by the way he was looking at her, his eyes honest and open and filled with something she couldn't recall ever seeing in a lover's face before. A look that somehow made her feel desired and cherished at the same time, stirring a breathless longing within her.

It was too much.

She wasn't ready to take that leap. She'd crashed

too many times already; she didn't think she could survive another one.

But no matter how hard she tried to convince herself, she couldn't walk away. Not with his eyes locked onto hers, telling her it would be different this time.

She dropped her gaze away from his eyes, hoping it would bring some relief, but it didn't help. All that did was bring his mouth into focus. They were in a secluded moonlit paradise, and his lips were only a breath away from hers.

"David..."

He bent towards her, stopping her words and making her forget the last of her objections. She melted into him, throwing her arms around his neck and sinking into his heat.

His kiss was nothing and everything like she had expected. He brushed her mouth with his, once - twice - silently asking her permission before going any farther.

In response, her hands delved into his hair, pulling him closer. She could feel his smile - or maybe it was her own - before his lips nudged hers again, seeking entrance. She gave it to him gladly, their tongues meeting in a dance of give and take.

At some point, he must have dropped his sword. One of his arms wrapped around her waist, holding her tight, while the other still rested on her face, his thumb tracing a seductive pattern on her cheek. She could feel his arm tightening around her, molding her body to his, and her own arms dropped, sliding from his hair and running down his broad shoulders to rest on his chest, his heart pounding madly under her fingertips.

Her hands drifted lower, trailing down his rock-hard stomach in a search for the bottom of his shirt. Finding the hem, she slipped her fingers up under the soft material.

She could feel the heat radiating from his skin. It seared her palms, leaving a tingling sensation behind that felt like fire dancing through her body. It was an intoxicating feeling, one she never wanted to end, even if it meant burning down the world around her. There was nothing that could stop her from diving headlong into the flames.

You have to tell him.

The tiny voice inside of her head cut through the fiery haze of her lust, chilling her with its cold rationality.

She was determined to ignore it. It couldn't possibly understand what it was asking her to give up.

Pretending her conscious had never spoken, she pressed into David, curling one leg around his calf and drawing him closer. In response, his hand dropped to her collarbone and his thumb began to caress her neck in a rhythmic stroke that was making her knees unsteady. His other hand slid around to caress her rear, his fingers splayed across her ass and molding her body tightly to his. Taking advantage of the position, she writhed slowly, savoring the friction they were generating between them.

Do you want to risk your curse hurting him? Do you

want to see him change and walk away?

Cassie was wrong. She wasn't going to ignore her subconscious. She was going to kill it. She was going to crush it under her heels, squishing it until it was little more than a splotch of goo, then she was going to scrape it off the bottom of her shoes and into a vat of acid.

She hated it for being right. She couldn't do this. Not to him.

Using every last ounce of willpower she had, she slipped her hands out from under his shirt and pushed lightly on his chest. "David, stop."

He pulled away immediately. "What's wrong? Are you okay?" He was breathing heavily, his lungs heaving in stuttered gasps, but he ignored his discomfort in his worry over her. "Oh God, I shouldn't have assumed... I don't know why I keep doing it..." He took an abrupt step backwards, almost tripping over his own feet in his haste to give her distance. "I promise it won't happen again."

Cassie hadn't thought she could get any warmer, but apparently, she was wrong. The temperature in her cheeks rose several degrees as she ducked her head to stare at the ground. "What if I want it to?" she mumbled.

"You do?" He sounded so surprised, she couldn't help but look.

He had stopped backing away. Instead, he seemed locked in place, frozen in a position somewhere between fleeing for safety and launching himself towards her.

She knew which one she'd prefer. Just the thought of being in his arms again… of feeling his lips scorching her skin as they ghosted over the arch of her neck…

She cleared her throat, trying not to sound as eager as she felt. "I… think so." Oh, who was she kidding? She'd give her left stiletto for a repeat performance. Hell, she'd be willing to give up her entire wardrobe. "I mean yes. Definitely yes."

"Oh." His body seemed to relax and a smile crept over his face. "Good. That's good. Really… really good. I'd like that."

"Yeah. Me too." The flush on her cheeks grew stronger. "But there's some things we should probably talk about first."

"You're right. We should be sensible about this. Use our heads. We wouldn't want to do anything we'd regret later." His breathing was still leveling out, making it hard to read his tone, but Cassie swore she could hear the same frustrated yearning she was feeling buried not far underneath its surface. "And this probably isn't the best time or place, either."

With the possibility of Nim eavesdropping on their every move? "Definitely not." Although seeing them together like that might be a good payback for the tricks the dryad had played on Cassie earlier. "There's other issues, too."

David nodded somberly. "I know. You still don't trust me."

"I'm trying to. It doesn't come easy for me."

"It's alright. I understand."

"I don't think you do." This was it. The perfect opportunity to tell him. So why couldn't she force the words out of her mouth?

She wasn't ready. What if he didn't want anything to do with her after he found out about her curse? What if he did? What if he cared enough to make the attempt and she ultimately drove him away anyway?

Terrified by the thought, she took the coward's way out. "I saw Gideon."

He took a step back, his eyes widening. "You did? Where?"

"Back at the house." She felt guilty using his brother to distract him, but she figured it was for the best. And at least it was good news. "That's why I'm in the forest. I followed him here."

"How is he? Is he okay?" The questions tumbled over each other. "What did he say?"

"Not much. From the little he told me, I think you were right about him hunting down his murderer. And I think you were right about something else. The zombies Striker and I ran into earlier weren't sentient. Judging by their clothes and their state of decay, they had to have been dead for years before resurrecting... which means someone had to have raised them."

David inhaled sharply, his face turning pale. "Do you think that person could have sent the zombie who attacked Sasha in the hospital?"

"Yes, and possibly the one in the original attack, as well." If Gideon had come back to avenge his murder, what reason could he have for going after Sasha and her companion? Neither had been anywhere near Scotland or Spain at the time of the accident, and Sasha had told the police she'd never met Gideon. "Maybe when they were camping, they stumbled across something they shouldn't have, and someone decided to remove them before they became a threat."

"Then that means Gideon isn't dangerous! I knew it!" He lurched forwards and swept Cassie up into a tight embrace. "He's going to be alright, and it's all thanks to you!" With one arm wrapped around her shoulders and the other snug around her waist, he lifted her off the ground and spun her around in celebration.

"I didn't do anything," she protested, trying not to laugh as he continued to twirl them, staring at her with his eyes shining with joy.

"Of course you did." He set her back down on the ground but didn't release her from his hold. "For the first time since this began, we have something to hope for." The arm around her shoulders shifted as he moved to caress her cheek. "And it wouldn't have happened without you."

"I don't know about that." She leaned into the caress, savoring the warmth of his touch. "I'm sure someone else would have figured it out... eventually."

His fingers dipped to her jawline, tracing the path from her ear to her chin. "Maybe. But no one else would have looked so beautiful doing it." With his fingers cradling her chin, he leaned forward until his lips were grazing her forehead. "Or felt so right in my arms," he whispered, the words causing tremors as they brushed against her skin, leaving her breathless.

She swallowed around the lump in her throat. "I suppose you're right."

"I am." He grinned, pulling back slightly. "But if you still need convincing..." His lips came down again, only this time it wasn't a gentle brush on her forehead.

His mouth claimed hers.

She gave in to his demand – and her own desire – and rose to meet him. Wrapping her arms around his neck, she pulled him closer, determined to make him feel the same desperate yearning he was causing her. Judging by the hungry growl issuing from his throat and way his fingers at her waist tightened with barely controlled restraint, she figured she was doing a pretty good job of it. It was hard to tell, though, considering her own head was swimming.

Lost in a wonderland of taste and touch, it took everything she had to break the kiss and pull away from him.

"Not that I'm not enjoying this..." she said, struggling to catch her breath. "But we did say we shouldn't rush into anything." *At least not until I talk to Ash and she tells me how to break the curse.* "And it is getting late. We should probably head back."

David immediately dropped his arms from around her and took a step back. "Right. Take it slow. No need to rush." His voice was rough, and Cassie noticed with a deep sense of satisfaction that he seemed to be having trouble focusing, his words coming out in uncoordinated bursts. "We should... find the path..."

He looked around, searching for the way out. "I know it was here somewhere." When he didn't find it, he took a deep breath and held it for a few seconds before slowly exhaling. "Maybe I should ask Nim for help."

"Maybe," Cass smirked, enjoying the sight of his discombobulation and the knowledge that she had caused it. "It's worth a shot." The dryad hadn't been willing to help Cassie out, but maybe she would listen to him.

He called to the dryad, and, of course, a path immediately opened up.

Wait a minute - does that mean the little wench was eavesdropping the whole time?

Finding herself in too good of a mood to care, Cassie waited for David to pick up his sword, and then they started back home, side by side. Not trusting herself to touch him without her hormones taking over, she kept a careful distance, putting a few inches between them to serve as a buffer.

As they walked along the path, neither one said much, limiting their conversation to occasional random comments scattered between long stretches of silence. It should have been awkward, but it wasn't. If anything, Cassie thought it was nice. It had been too long since she'd felt the strange combination of excitement and nerves that came with the start of a new relationship. By the time they got back to the house, it was all she could do to keep the stupid grin off her face.

Luckily, there was someone waiting there to wipe it off. The Englishman, Charles, was lurking inside the entranceway, and apparently something had put him in a foul mood. His lips were drawn in a sardonic twist and there was disdain in his pale blue eyes.

"Ah, I see the conquering heroine has deemed to grace us with her presence," he said, lifting a glass of amber colored liquor up in a half-hearted salute. "The world may now resume its previously arranged orbit."

Ignoring the temptation to hit him hard enough to send him into an orbit of his own, Cassie bit her tongue and tried to remain polite. "What do you want, Charlie?"

"Nothing much. Although perhaps it would be nice if you could inform our hosts you're here so that we may finally sit down to dinner." He took a gulp of his drink, swaying slightly on his feet. "They've been holding it for over an hour."

David stepped forward. "Sorry about that. We lost track of the time." He flushed, stealing a glance Cassie's way. "I'll let them know we're back." He put his hand on the small of her back and drew close enough to whisper in her ear. "Don't worry; I won't tell them why we were late." His breath ghosted against her skin, sending a barely concealed shiver coursing down her spine. "Although they'll probably figure it out for themselves when they realize I can't stop smiling when I look at you."

"Then don't look at me."

"I'll hold out for as long as I can, but I'm not making any promises. I don't seem to have any will power when it comes to resisting you." He straightened up with a grin. "Until dinner, then, Ms. Jones."

After a polite nod to Charles, he made his way out of the room.

I'm not going to watch him go... I'm not going to watch him go...

She was a professional, damn it, not a lovesick schoolgirl. She didn't need to take every chance she could get to see him.

She made it to the count of three before she turned.

The rear view was just as delectable as the front one. The way the seat of his pants clung to his ass, muscles shifting as he walked, was a work of art...

And now that she knew what those muscles felt like under her hands? She didn't know how much longer she was going to be able to wait.

What was taking Ash so long?

I should give her a call.

"Miss Jones..."

But if I interrupt her, she'll have less time to get information... and speaking of calling, I've got to call for another copy of the mechanic's report...

"Miss Jones!" A sharp voice barked out.

She looked up to see the Englishman staring at her.

"What?"

"I would like to request a moment of your time."

"Sure. I have some free time tomorrow. I'll pencil you in for 10 AM." *Wait... isn't there a time difference between here and home? Maybe that's why Ash hasn't called.*

"I meant I would like to request your time now. If it's convenient, of course."

"Tomorrow would be better." She was sure she'd hear back from Ash by then, and she'd be far less distracted. She'd be more prepared to deal with whatever it was Charlie wanted to discuss. "Today's been a long day."

"I'm sorry," he said, wearing an expression that showed absolutely no remorse. "But I simply must insist."

"So, it's not so much of a request as a demand," she pointed out. When he didn't even have the grace to look embarrassed, she heaved a deep sigh. "Fine. But make it quick."

"I suppose I should start with an apology. I know I can be abrasive when I'm hungry. Never-the-less, I wanted to tell you how impressed I am with your handling of this case."

"Gee, thanks. You can't imagine how much that means to me."

"When I first heard you were coming here, I didn't have very high expectations for your success," he continued. "I'd never heard of you, you see, and you *are* an American. Still, you've been here less than twenty-four hours and you've already managed to find and eliminate the zombies who attacked poor

Miss Kramer and her companion."

"No. I didn't."

"Don't be modest. You aren't going to tell me Striker saved you, are you? I find that hard to believe since he's the one lying upstairs in a state of compos de-mentis."

"I wasn't going to say that. I did take care of the zombies that attacked us, but they weren't the ones who attacked Miss Kramer."

"Really?" The Englishman asked with a look of profound skepticism. "How can you be sure?"

"Because the three that attacked Striker and I weren't capable of much more than basic motor skills. If they had a brain between them it was because they found one they were trying to eat."

"What difference does that make?"

"To sneak in and out of the hospital without drawing any attention to himself, a zombie would have to have some level of conscious thought. If he didn't, instead of searching out her room, he would have treated the place like an all-you-can-eat buffet."

"So her attacker was sentient then... just as Gideon would be."

"Not likely. A totally mindless zombie wouldn't have got in there at all, but a fully sentient one would have waited until the hospital was less crowded to attack... which means someone was controlling it. And if it was under someone's control, chances are good that the zombie who attacked the campsite was too, and that he'll attack again."

Charles blanched at her words, his pasty skin

turning even paler. "I must say, you do know quite a bit about zombies, don't you?"

"That's my job. I'm a hunter."

"You're quite good at it." Charles paused and she began to hope she was finally going to be free of him, but apparently he had just been working up the courage to ask her something. "Which brings me to about to the reason I wanted to speak to you. I was hoping you might permit me to accompany you the next time you go out hunting."

"Why?"

"I've done a lot of studies on the paranormal, but I've had very little field research with zombies. I believe it would be beneficial for me to get a more fleshed-out view of them, if you'll pardon the pun."

"I'm sorry, but it would be too dangerous to have you along."

It was true. She would kill him if she had to spend any time with him.

"I assure you I wouldn't be any bother. In fact, I often accompanied Gideon on his paranormal wildlife expeditions."

Wait... had Charlie finally managed to say something useful?

"Did you just say Gideon was exploring the paranormal?"

The Englishman nodded emphatically, puffing up at the opportunity to boast. "Oh yes, he went all the time and I often accompanied him. In fact, I was supposed to go with him right before he died, but the expedition needed to be rescheduled when he took over for David on the trip to Spain."

"Excuse me?" She couldn't have heard that right. "David was supposed to go to Spain... not Gideon?"

"Yes, didn't you know? David was originally supposed to go on that trip, but something came up at the last minute and his brother filled in for him."

"No, I didn't."

David had lied to her.

Again.

Chapter Nine

Cassie leaned back against the cool porcelain of her Olympic-sized bathtub, a pile of frothy bubbles surrounding her and the scent of heather and honey deluging her senses. On a small table placed thoughtfully nearby, a plate of mouth-watering hors d'oeuvres rested alongside a brimming mug of hot tea liberally spiked with whiskey. After talking to Charlie, there was no way she could have faced David across the dinner table, so she'd pled fatigue and had a tray sent to her room. Her hosts had been nothing but sympathetic, sending up everything they thought she might possibly want.

She hadn't been able to take a bite of it.

Maybe he hadn't lied. Maybe he had forgotten. It'd be an easy enough mistake to make. It could happen to anyone.

Yeah, right. She couldn't believe she'd almost fallen for it. How could she have been so stupid?

She dunked her loofah under the soapy water, imagining it was David's neck and wringing it viscously.

Anger was good. Anger drove away the pain she felt every time she remembered how close she had come to believing.

She threw the mutilated loofah in the trash and pulled the tub's plug.

The water swirled down the drain with a loud sucking gurgle. Wrapping one of the plush Egyptian cotton towels around her body and another around her hair, she stomped out of the bathroom and collapsed on top of her bed in an ungainly sprawl.

It was for the best. Tomorrow was a new day, and when it dawned, Cassie would be back to her old self, focused solely on the case. No more letting herself be distracted by a pair of warm brown eyes and the promise of a dream that could never come true.

And if tonight she indulged herself in a few tears and most of the bottle of scotch, she'd never let him know.

***

Morning came, and even if her eyes were puffy and her head pounded, the world hadn't ended, so she threw on some makeup to hide the damage, popped a few ibuprofen, and headed to the breakfast salon.

It was exactly what she would expect from something called 'the breakfast salon.' Sumptuously decorated, it boasted an elaborate Mahogany sideboard and a gilded serving set. In fact, everything appeared to be gilded, from the delicate porcelain teacups up to and including the server hovering anxiously over warming trays filled with various delicacies.

The only other people in the room were David's father and two of the resident scientists. One of them, a middle-aged man with crumbs in his bushy gray beard, was in an animated conversation with Mr. MacDuff. The second was Charlie, looking only marginally more sober than he had the night before.

He rose as she entered the room, pulling out a chair adjacent to his.

"It appears you've had a rough night," he commented as he catalogued the dark circles under Cassie's eyes and the red lines running through them.

Against her better judgment, she took the proffered seat. "I'll give you a thousand dollars if you stop talking now."

The server she had noticed earlier placed a plate in front of her, loaded with what appeared to be Eggs Benedict drenched in Hollandaise, potatoes O'Brien, and fresh melon.

"Nonsense," Charles insisted. "A little food and some good company will set you to rights. Trust me, I know whereof I speak."

He did look positively cheerful for someone who had drunk so much the night before.

Probably because he's still drunk.

Still, the food did look good. She picked up the melon and took a cautious bite. It didn't cause her stomach to rebel, so she cut into the eggs. As the yolk broke and flowed down to mingle with the buttery sauce, the lingering remnants of her hangover began to disappear.

"You see, I'm always right," he said pompously.

"Uh-huh," Cassie muttered around a mouthful of perfectly toasted English muffin coated liberally with the Hollandaise/egg mixture. She wondered if it would be possible to get more of the sauce to pour on top of the potatoes.

She looked up to make sure the server was still nearby. She didn't want him going too far before she got a second helping.

"So," Charles inquired, spewing his noxious breath directly into Cassie's face and causing her stomach to turn over rebelliously, "There's a rumour going around that you won't be hunting Gideon after all."

Cassie scowled. "The rumors are wrong."

"Come now," the Englishman persisted. "You can tell me. You said it yourself, Gideon didn't attack Miss Kramer, so you can let him be."

If Mr. MacDuff had missed the mention of Gideon's name the first time, he caught it now. "Is that true? Gideon is going to be alright?" In the bright sunlight streaming in through the high arched windows, his unruly orange hair formed a bright halo around his head. Combined with the hopeful smile he wore, it gave him the appearance of a cheerful cherub.

She wished she didn't have to take that hope away.

"No. I'm sorry, but it's not true. Gideon might not be responsible for this attack, but he's still a zombie. It won't be his fault, but eventually, he's going to lose control."

Malcolm's face fell. "I had hoped…"

Shit. This is what she had been trying to avoid.

Before she could figure out how to ease his pain, Malcolm spoke again. "I understand. You do what you need to do. You have our full support."

Cassie watched in disbelief as he rose from his seat and crossed to her.

"I can't tell you how much it means to me - how much it means to us all - to have you here." Taking one of her hands in both of his, he gave it a comforting squeeze. "Gideon would never forgive himself if he hurt an innocent person. In my heart, I can't help but think he would agree with you."

He raised her hand to his lips, brushing it with a gentle kiss. "I believe he would have liked you very much. I know we all do."

Why the hell would he say something like that? I should be trying to make him feel better, not the other way around.

There was only one answer – he was crazy. They were all crazy, and they were trying to make her crazy, too.

She had to get out of here. She needed to solve the case and then get her ass out of the MacDuff madhouse. They all seemed intent on throwing her off-balance and threatening the equilibrium it had taken her years to learn.

As if he could sense her distress, Charles leaned over to whisper in her ear.

"I think you need something stronger than sugar for your tea." He pulled a flask from an inner pocket of his suit coat. "Just say the word."

It's too much. I can't do this anymore.

Pushing her chair back from the table, she sprung to her feet. "I've got to get to work. Please tell the chef that breakfast was delicious."

Mr. MacDuff started to say something, but she rushed out of the room before he could get any words out. She didn't want to hear it. He was just like his son... plying her with pretty words and compliments that didn't mean anything...treating her like she meant something to them...

There had to be a reason they were doing it. They had to be hiding something. But what?

At least there was one person she could count on to tell her the truth.

She asked one of the maids wandering around the castle where she could find him, and within two minutes, she was at Striker's door.

She tapped on it lightly, not wanting to disturb him if he was asleep.

"Come in," a feminine voice called out.

Cassie opened the door to see Diana MacDuff sitting in a chair alongside Striker's bed. He was awake and, judging from the semi-empty plates littering the tray beside him, he had just finished eating breakfast.

"Cassie, how wonderful," Diana exclaimed with a pleased smile. "I'm going to have to leave shortly, but I was worried about leaving Striker alone. Do you think you'd be able to sit with him for a while until I get back?"

"Of course." She didn't know if the woman was in on whatever her son and husband were up to, but she didn't want to take any chances. She needed to talk to Striker privately.

"Thank you so much. I can't tell you how much you've relieved my mind. And I know Striker will be grateful for the company, won't you, dear?"

Striker's answer was a noncommittal grunt.

Diana didn't seem bothered by his lack of response. She fluffed his pillows and made sure he had a fresh pitcher of water on the table beside him before gathering up the remnants of his breakfast and loading them on a tray. "Just let me know if there's anything you need." After one last check to make sure he was comfortable, she made her way out, the door closing behind her with a quiet click.

The sound seemed to act as a catalyst, prodding Striker to break his self-imposed silence. "You should have listened to me when I told you to run." He wasn't looking at her, his eyes closed and his head tilted back against the propped-up pillows behind his back. He had a small strip of gauze wrapped around his forehead, but it wasn't as bad as Cassie had feared. He probably wouldn't even get a scar from it.

"I got us out of there, didn't I?" she said.

"You got lucky." His voice floated up towards the ceiling, completely devoid of any gratitude. "Those zombies could have killed you."

Not likely. If the blowtorch hadn't worked, they still would have had to get past her machete and her grenades. Not to mention her shoes. "So, how are you feeling?"

"Like I got hit in the head with a machete. Can't

imagine why."

"I'd say I was sorry, but you deserved it. Why would you think it was a good idea to run from a zombie? You had to have known it would chase you."

"Uh-huh. Straight away from you."

Oh.

She supposed she shouldn't be surprised. She'd met Striker's type before. Hell, she'd dated his type before, more times than she cared to remember. The type that might not use pretty words, but that would lay their lives down without a second thought.

The type of man she could trust.

"I talked to Charlie."

Striker didn't bother to move. "And?"

"Gideon wasn't supposed to go on that trip to Spain, was he?"

"Are you asking or telling me?"

"I think you already know. And I'm hoping you can tell me why they made the change." Her fingernails dug into her palms as she waited for the answer that would either condemn or clear David.

Striker's eyes remain closed. "Don't know. One minute Dave was packing his bags to go, the next, it was Gideon."

Damn.

She pulled her chair closer to the bed. "Do you think he had something to do with his brother's death?"

He finally opened his eyes, but he didn't say anything. He just kept staring at her, his face completely blank. She was about to give up and ask him something else when his answer came. "I wish I could say no, but I can't."

Damn. Damn. Damn.

Pain shot through her, starting in the pit of her stomach and spreading throughout her until she felt nauseous. "Why not?"

Striker shifted in the bed. "It's probably nothing. It's not like I've got any proof or anything. Just a gut feeling."

"About what?"

"He's been... different lately."

"His brother died and came back as a zombie." She wasn't looking for excuses for him. She wasn't. "That could make anyone act a little strange."

"Before that. Even as a kid, he followed his brother around like a shadow, doing whatever Gideon wanted to do. At the time, he seemed happy about it, but for the past two years..."

"What changed?"

"He started acting weird. Started distancing himself from Gideon and me and keeping secrets." He shook his head, his brows drawn together in what looked to be an uncomfortable memory. "He'd disappear for days, sometimes weeks. Even after his brother died and he was supposed to be running the company, there'd be times when no one had any idea how to find him." Striker met Cassie's eyes directly. "The way I figure it is, he's got a reason for disappearing the way he does. And I'm thinking it has something to do with the special project Gideon was working on."

A special project?

Cassie sat up, homing in on the new information like a dragon spotting an unclaimed pile of gold. "Mr. MacDuff said Gideon wasn't working on anything. So did you when I first questioned you."

"He didn't want to tell his family about it until it was finished. And I didn't know if I could trust you or not." He looked as if he still hadn't made up his mind about it.

"Do you have any idea what it was?"

"No. I kept out of the inventing side of things. That was Gideon's job. It was my job to protect him, to make sure nothing stopped him from fulfilling his work." Striker's hands clenched into tight fists. "But he died anyway, and sometimes I wonder if David had something to do with it." With a visible effort, he forced his hands to relax. "Not that I expect you to believe anything I say against him. I know you're interested in him."

She placed her hand on Striker's wrist to make sure she had his full attention. "David is my employer. Nothing else." There was no point in wishing otherwise. "My only interest in him is regarding the case."

His face as his eyes dropped to where her hand rested, then lifted again to meet hers. "Are you sure about that?"

"Positive."

"I was hoping you'd say that." Grabbing her wrist, he pulled her off-balance, causing her to sprawl against his chest.

She almost jerked away from him before telling herself she didn't have any reason to resist. This was the kind of guy she should be going after. Not the kind who opened doors and waited for permission to kiss her - all while keeping secrets from her.

With her hands splayed against the bed, she leaned in closer. Striker smelled like musk and leather and wood burning in an open fire, nothing like cool autumn wind. His arms surrounded her and his tongue invaded the recesses of her mouth. In response, she threw everything she had into it, using all the tricks she had ever learned.

Nothing. Absolutely nothing. He was everything she could hope for, but he didn't give her butterflies.

What the hell was wrong with her?

Reluctantly, she broke the kiss. It wouldn't be fair to either of them to continue when she wasn't into it. "Striker... stop."

He moved to her neck, biting just hard enough to leave a faint mark.

"You're sure?" He slid his hands down to her ass. "If you're worried about my injuries, I promise I'm healthy enough for anything you care to do."

She pushed his hands aside. "It's not that." Outside, something must have brushed up against the window, hitting it with a jarring noise. "It's nothing against you." She maneuvered herself up to a sitting position. "I think we'd be better off keeping this strictly business, okay?"

He shrugged and put his arms behind his head.

"If that's how you want it."

"It is." Another rap at the window sounded. "What the hell is that?"

She went to the window and drew the curtains aside.

Outside, an elm tree was swaying in the wind, its limbs striking angrily against the windowpane.

They should really have someone look at that. If the wind picks up, it could shatter the glass.

She was just about to let the drapes fall closed when something caught the corner of her eye.

David was walking quickly through the garden, occasionally glancing over his shoulder and carrying an oddly shaped package that resembled nothing so much as a longsword.

What is he doing?

"Something wrong?" Striker's voice came from the bed. He struggled to sit up.

Shit.

Cassie knew he wanted to help, but he was going to reinjure himself. If she took the time to convince him to stay put, she'd lose David's trail.

Thinking quickly, she reached up and removed the curtain sash, letting the drapes fall closed. With the thickly woven cord and its tasseled fringes draped across her palm in a silken cascade, she stalked back to the bed and knelt on the mattress.

"You change your mind? Can't say I'm sorry." He held his wrists out eagerly and Cassie bound them together before lashing them to the headboard. "Not my usual style, but I try to be accommodating."

After testing to make sure the knot was sturdy, Cassie sat back on her heels and surveyed her work.

Yep, that'll do.

"I'm sorry, Striker," she said, vaulting off the bed, "but I've got to go. I've got a lead to follow, and you'd just slow me down."

She crossed to the window and opened the sash, ignoring the protests coming from behind her. "I'll send someone to untie you, I promise."

Cassie's dress kept hiking up to her waist, and her hair caught in the elm's branches at least ten or twenty times, but at least her shoes were safe. She held them aloft in one hand so she wouldn't scuff the heels on tree bark. As she worked her way down to the ground, she could hear Striker angrily yelling at her to come back and let him out. She had to admire his vocabulary – some of the names he called her were truly inventive.

Truthfully, though, she didn't think he had a right to be upset. She had tied him to the bed for his own good. He'd received a head wound. Who knew what would happen to him if she let him come along now?

Finally reaching the ground, she slipped her heels back on and started running. David had a head start on her, but she felt confident she could catch up to him. She had done far too many summers' worth of endurance training at Ash's house to lose easily.

Staying far enough back that he wouldn't see her, she watched as he moved in the direction of the lake she had seen when she first arrived.

He circled around it, cutting through shrubs and bushes and disturbing the sprites living in them, but as fast as he was walking, he didn't manage to widen the gap between himself and Cassie. He led her past the lake, through a grassy clearing and towards another section of forest that looked like a wilderness path. More specifically, the kind of path designed by bored Victorian landowners to give themselves a private place to fool around with the help without being seen.

If David got there before her, she was going to lose sight of him.

He sped up and Cassie put out a burst of speed, deepening her breathing to get the extra oxygen her body required to maintain the higher pace.

It wasn't enough. He slipped into the forest and disappeared into the woods.

Damn it. Had he spotted her?

She slowed down, unwilling to go charging into an ambush.

At least this forest didn't seem as hostile as the previous one. Either it was out of the dryad's territory or her attention was elsewhere. Whatever the reason was, Cassie was grateful. She'd take any advantage she could get.

She had to admit, he was surprisingly good. He was fast, and he knew enough not to leave obvious clues about which way he had gone. But he hadn't managed to hide everything. He must have picked up some mud on the bottom of his shoes from the area around the lake, and as it dried, it was flaking off, leaving an almost invisible trail. She followed it as far as she could. By the time the trail dried up completely, she had come to the other side of the woods.

Stepping out of it, she could see a small stone cottage approximately ten meters away. It was disgustingly cute, with smoke curling from its chimney and wildflowers surrounding its foundation. Ivy vines crawled up its whitewashed walls, and birds were singing cheerful songs from their perches on the thatched roof.

If seven freaking dwarves show up, I am so out of here.

There was no sign of David, but she knew he had to be here somewhere. Unless he had doubled back into the forest, he was in or around the cottage. She checked the perimeter first. She couldn't find any signs of him, and there was nothing out of the ordinary. Had he gone in? And if he had, was there anybody else in there with him?

What is this place, and why is he hiding it?

She crept to one of the windows and cautiously peered in.

The first window she checked revealed an unoccupied bedroom. It was spartan, with only a heavy wooden bed covered in a thick quilt that looked to be handmade. She moved on to the next window to find a room almost identical to the first. The only difference was the color of the bedspread, this one a deep burgundy as opposed to the previous navy blue.

At the third window, she struck gold.

At one time, it must have served as the main

room of the house. She imagined it had been used for welcoming guests or doing the daily crossword puzzle – whatever it was people who didn't chase zombies for a living did for relaxation.

Whatever it had been before, it served a different purpose now. Cleared of all furniture, it had a thin wide mat that spread over most of the floor. Racks of weapons lined all four sides of the room. Battle-axes, scimitars, maces and broadswords; it looked as if every kind of weapon known to man was in there.

Cassie knew a war room when she saw one.

What is he planning on doing with all of this?

As she craned her neck to try and see more of the room, Cassie heard someone moving around inside. She ducked down, trying to stay out of sight. She was debating whether she should try the other windows for a better view or if she should go inside now when the decision was taken from her. The front door was creaking open.

Moving as quickly as she could without giving her presence away, she hurried around the corner towards the front of the house.

His back towards her and he was standing less than a foot away, locking the door. The sword shaped package was gone, but he still stood as if he was ready to move at a moment's notice, distributing his weight equally between his feet in a fighter's stance.

A moment's unease crept through her. Was it David or Gideon?

It was too hard to tell from this angle.

As she watched, he dropped the key into the back pocket of his pants.

"Stop right where you are," she warned him, inching forward. "We need to talk. How 'bout you turn around nice and easy, now? And keep your hands in the air, please."

He lifted his arms high above his head, pivoting slowly until he faced her. "Cassie, sweetheart, what are you doing here?"

Cassie scowled. It was definitely David, not Gideon. No one else would have the nerve to call her sweetheart while lying right to her face.

At least she had caught him red-handed this time. "Just open the door."

"Cass, what's wrong?" he asked, looking bewildered. "Has something happened?"

Oh, he was damned good, all right. Without the proof right before her eyes, she might think he was telling the truth.

"Nice try." She didn't know if he was trying to hurt Gideon or if the two were working together in some convoluted scheme, but either way, she was going to put an end to it and see they both got what they deserved. "I followed you here from the castle. I want to know what this place is."

David flushed guiltily. "I can explain everything. If you'll just come inside..." He fished the key out of his pocket and unlocked the door.

Cassie clutched his arm, preventing him from stepping through the doorway.

"Don't even think about it. Until I know exactly

what – or who – is waiting in there, I don't want you out of my sight."

She pulled him beside her, ignoring the puzzled look he was giving her. If only she could ignore the way having him this close made her pulse jump. "Just do everything I tell you to do and don't say a word."

He nodded, silently.

They made their way through the entranceway and into the main room. Surrounded by racks of weapons, Cassie did a quick survey. Once she found what she was looking for, she dragged him over and picked up a gleaming Lochaber ax with a sturdy haft. "This will do nicely." Much more cheerful now that she was appropriately armed, she pulled him through the rest of the house.

They explored each room, checking high and low. *Nothing.* No sign that Gideon or anyone else was in residence. The windows were locked shut from the inside, proving he couldn't have made his escape that way, and there were no doors other than the front one.

She ended her search in the kitchen. A small room, it contained little more than a white porcelain stove, a cast iron sink, and a wooden table.

As she took a second to debate her next move, David spoke for the first time since they had entered the cottage. "Cassie, what is this about?" He hadn't made any move to break free from her grip, but he was watching her with a wounded look in his eyes.

The asshole.

She dropped her grip on his arm, unable to bear the thought of touching him. "Awfully nice arsenal you've got here. Care to tell me about it?"

He flinched.

She sank into one of the chairs, wanting to see the look on his face as he tried to lie his way out of this one. "So, what's with all the weapons? Are you planning on starting some sort of war? Did Gideon find out about it? Is that why you killed him?"

"It's not what it looks like." When Cassie only stared back at him, he let out a heavy sigh and pulled a chair away from the table.

He sat down. "This is Gideon's place. He used to come here whenever he could find a spare moment. He said he did his best thinking when he was training."

Cassie laughed skeptically. "Are you trying to tell me this was his exercise studio?"

"Sort of." One shoulder rose in an embarrassed half-shrug. "I guess you could call it more of a dojo than anything else. He'd practice different styles of fighting here; he thought it helped sharpen his mind. Sometimes he'd talk me into joining him and we'd do a little sparring. You wouldn't believe how good he was." His eyes lit up, and she had to remind herself that his innocence and the 'aw, shucks' routine he was dishing out were all an act.

"I did manage to surprise him once or twice," he continued, "but I always figured he let me win." His arm stretched across the table, reaching for her hand. "I came here this morning because I needed to figure some things out. It worked for Gideon; I guess I was hoping it would work for me, too."

She had to give him credit. The rich warmth of his voice was calling out to her, begging her to believe him. If she didn't know better, she'd think he was actually sincere.

Staring dismissively at his outstretched hand, she folded her arms across her chest. "So that's it? You just needed some 'you time'?"

He shifted uncomfortably, dropping his hand. "Not entirely." The tips of his fingers dug into the tabletop, leaving faint marks. "I came here because I thought Gideon might be here. I didn't tell you about it because I didn't want you to find him yet."

Finally, we're getting somewhere - and all it took was catching him in yet another lie.

"Why not?"

"Even if we can prove Gideon's innocent, it's not going to change things, is it? You're still going to help him die again."

"Isn't that what you wanted?" Her chin lifted in challenge. "It's why you hired me in the first place."

"I know." His fingers spasmed, digging deeper into the wood. His eyes fell and, with a visible start, he noticed the damage he had done to the table. Grimacing, he moved his hands to his lap, where his fingers dug into his thighs. "That was before I realized he hadn't attacked anyone." His grip tightened hard enough to turn his knuckles white. "You don't have to kill him, Cassie. He's not a danger to anyone."

Cassie stared at him, trying to judge his sincerity as her mind raced frantically in what felt like a thousand different directions.

He's telling the truth. You can believe him.

She wanted to. God, she wanted to. But what about the lies he'd already told? Hiding the truth about his brother's murder... the existence of this place... the last-minute switch in travel plans...

"I already gave you a second chance. That's more then I give most people."

"I was going to tell you about the cottage. I just wanted to talk to Gideon first."

"Uh-huh. And when were you going to tell me that Gideon took your place on the trip to Spain?"

He pulled back in surprise. "What?"

"Gideon was never supposed to go on that trip. You were... until you called off at the last minute. Pretty convenient, that."

"Do you really think I would..." he ran his fingers roughly through his hair. "Cassie, I didn't mention it because I didn't think it was important. Five minutes after it happened, I had forgotten all about it."

"Yeah, right." *How many more chances am I supposed to give? How many risks do I take before I finally learn my lesson?*

He leaned forward in his seat, pleading. "Just give me a little time to prove what I'm saying."

No. She couldn't do it. Even if he was telling the truth, she couldn't let this happen. Fairy tales didn't come true. The serving girl might end up with a prince, but Cassie was never going to get a happy ending. Neither would Gideon. It'd be better for everyone to accept that now.

She stood up. "You can fire me if you want to, but I'm going to find him anyway." David looked like he was going to argue, so she cut him off. "Stay out of my way or I'll take you down, too. Oh, and there's one other thing I think we should get clear." She forced the words past the sudden lump in her throat. "We need to stop this thing between us."

"This thing?"

"Yeah, you know. The fooling around. I mean, sure, it's been interesting, but work is work and lust is lust, and never the twain shall meet, right?"

He flinched as if he'd been hit by one of the poleaxes lined up against the wall in the other room. "Lust?" he asked. "Is that all it was?"

"Of course," she laughed, wondering if it sounded as false to his ears as it did to hers. "What else would it be? Which is not to say I didn't enjoy it." She ran her hand along the mark Striker had left on her throat, drawing David's attention to it. "I can't decide who more fun... you or Striker."

"Glad I could be of service." His words were clipped, and the vulnerability had disappeared from his eyes, leaving them cold and distant. "If we're done here, I should be going. I've wasted enough of your time."

Swallowing down the urge to tell him she was wrong, that she had changed her mind, she nodded. "Yeah. We're done."

As she watched him walk away, she told herself it was for the best.

Chapter Ten

Roses are red, Violets are blue; if you weren't lucky, the Cataclysm screwed you.

***

"No," Cassie said angrily as she threw another stack of papers onto the crumpled heap behind her. "Not this one either."

After watching David walk away, she'd had two choices. She could chase after him and tell him she was sorry and hadn't meant any of what she said, or she could ignore the way her heart felt like it was cracking in two and get on with her job.

Choosing work was safe. It had never betrayed her.

So why did she almost run out the door after him?

In the end, she'd forced herself to make the smart decision. She would put David out of her mind and use the afternoon to investigate reports of zombie sightings or unusual occurrences in the past few years.

She made her way to the local police office - or,

if she was going to be precise, a dusty room in the basement of the local police office - and so far, she'd gone through half the file cabinet without finding anything. Who knew there'd be so many reports of paranormal activity in a place like this?

David would know. He could help us. He said he would help us.

He said a lot of things.

Maybe he was telling the truth.

Maybe he wasn't.

Tired of the argument circling endlessly in her head, she turned back to scanning the reports. She could discount most of them immediately. Ghost chickens periodically harassing a luckless poultry rancher; a headless horseman showing up shortly after a group of teenage kids had stolen and consumed an entire keg of beer from the Sleepy Hollow pub; and a poltergeist that kept trying to file an eviction notice against a wraith who had taken up residence in his house. All the reports were normal run-of-the-mill occurrences. She rifled through them all with a growing frustration.

There was nothing here. She'd wasted half the day for nothing.

"Hang on. This one could prove interesting." The report in her hands was from sixteen months ago. It described an itinerant salesman who had been arrested for suspicion of vandalism and trespassing on private land. Cassie couldn't put her finger on it, but something about this file was pulling at her. She wasn't sure why - there wasn't a lot of information, and it didn't have any mention of zombies - but her instincts were screaming she had found what she was looking for.

Reading it more closely, she discovered the incident had occurred in an abandoned barn thirty miles away. Before the cataclysm, there had been rumors the barn was haunted, but nothing had been reported to the police until four years ago. That's when the activity had become more frequent. People passing by would hear strange noises and see flashing lights. Two years ago, one individual had reported smelling a strange metallic odor in the air. When police went to investigate, they had found cold spots, electrical interference, and an asymmetrically stacked pile of lumber – all classic signs of paranormal activity

Determining that whatever was there was not creating a public danger, they had granted the unseen specter full squatter's rights under the Supernatural Residency Act of 2039 and left it to go about its business. After that, the incidents increased, but people paid little to no attention to them.

Then, shortly over a year ago, an elderly couple living nearby had spotted a shabbily dressed individual skulking around the barn. The intruder had been arrested and brought to the jailhouse. He had been kept overnight, but the next day had been released on bail. The charges against him were dropped when the barn's spectral inhabitant didn't turn up to press charges.

Why is this important? What does it have to do with anything?

She flipped back to the front page of the report, staring at the docket number and the rest of the official information.

"John Green... why does that sound so familiar?"

A light clicked on in her head. John Green... also known as Sasha Kramer's boyfriend. The same man who had been killed in the zombie attack at the campground.

Which meant he'd been here before. And if he'd been here before, chances are he knew someone in the area.

If she could find who that person was, she could be halfway to solving the case. Luckily, she'd knew exactly where to look.

She started pulling the filing cabinets' heavy drawers open, unsure which one held what she was looking for. "DUIs, Domestic Abuse, Burglaries..." she was getting closer... "Bail bonds! Got it."

From personal experience, Cassie knew that when you got thrown in jail, even if it was for a perfectly innocent act which you may or may not have committed under the influence of a staggering amount of alcohol, there was one thing you were gonna do.

You would call a friend to come bail you out.

And the name scrawled at the bottom of John's paperwork was...

Well now, isn't that interesting?

***

"Perfect," Cassie exclaimed as she strode into the room where lunch was being served. An altogether different room from the dining room or the breakfast salon, she might add.

How many rooms do these people have for food anyway?

Cassie wasn't sure, but she had to say she approved of this one. With its cheerful yellow curtains and its heaping platters of food, it had everything Cassie needed.

Including the Englishman who was going to give her some answers.

"Just the man I was looking for," she said, grabbing three or four sandwiches and piling them on a plate before sitting down next to him.

Charles looked up from his own lunch - a bowl of soup and an anemic-looking salad he was staring at like it held the secrets of the universe. "Me?" he asked querulously. "Whatever for?" His eyes were bloodshot, his skin was pale and puffy, and he kept rubbing his forehead with one hand as if he could make his headache magically disappear.

Apparently, his hangover had finally caught up with him.

"Do I need a reason to talk to my favorite Englishman?" She asked loudly, enjoying the sight of him wincing in pain. "I thought we were friends."

"Yes, yes, of course." He dropped his head to his plate again, listlessly stirring his soup in a clockwise motion. "Friends…"

"I'm glad to hear it, old buddy," she said, clapping him roughly on the back.

His body jerked forward, his spoon going flying and leaving a trail of split-pea-colored droplets scattered over the pristine white tablecloth. "Why are you doing this to me?"

Cassie struggled to hide her grin. "Doing what, Charlie? Is something wrong? Maybe some food will help. I saw some tuna fish salad over there that doesn't smell too ripe. I could get you some of that. Or we could find out if there's any Haggis available. I've heard it can cure all sorts of ills." She took an enthusiastic bite of her own sandwich.

"Please, stop," he begged, his face turning a lovely shade of green that was almost a perfect match for his soup. "Just stop talking."

"Sure, I'll stop talking, Charlie," Cassie boomed, pulling up every bit of vocal projection she was capable of. "If you'll just tell me one little thing."

His hands came up to shield his ears, his eyelids at half-mast. "What?" he whined in a piteous voice, "What do you want? I'll tell you anything you want to know as long as you promise to… stop… talking."

Fun and games done… it was time to get serious. She lowered her voice and whispered into Charles' ear. "I want you to tell me exactly how you and Gideon knew John Green."

"I have no idea what you're talking about."

"Oh really?" If he wanted to play dumb, she was going to have to be vicious.

She could live with that.

"Then I guess I'll just have to send for that haggis. I hear the cook makes it with extra helpings of sheep lung. And she doesn't skimp on the hearts, either." She made smacking noises with her mouth, letting him get the full picture in his mind. "Sounds tasty."

Charlie groaned. Red splotches were mixing with the green already showing on his face, giving him an uncanny resemblance to a Christmas tree. "I'm telling you the truth, I swear," he stammered frantically. "I've never heard the name before."

He sounded convincing, but she knew better. "Then why did you and Gideon bail him out of jail?" He still looked confused, so she continued. "Almost two years ago... he was arrested for trespassing..." she prodded.

"I did?" He looked more befuddled than ever. "Are you sure?"

"Completely." Gideon's signature had been on the bail bond. So had the releasing officer's name. Cassie had managed to track the policeman down and question him about that night. He didn't remember much, but what he did recall was that Gideon and John had acted like good friends, greeting each other with what seemed to be mutual trust and affection. Maybe more importantly, the officer was able to tell Cassie there had been someone else who had come along with Gideon.

Judging by the description he had given – tall, lanky, obnoxious, and drunk – it could only have been Charles. "You and Gideon went to the jail to get him out."

Charles blinked, his watery eyes showing a faint sense of recognition. "Oh, him. Was his name John? I always thought it was Geoffrey." He shook his head. "He looked like a Geoffrey. I'm positive he was one."

Cassie reeled him in before he could wander off the subject. "Then you do know him?" she asked patiently.

"Not well." He was resuming his normal color, the mottled greens and reds fading to a warmer beige. "I believe he sold designer amphiphilic polymers."

"Amphi-whatic polymers?"

"Amphiphilic polymers," he repeated. "They're used mostly as emulsifiers and in pharmaceutical applications. The company Geoffrey worked for held the patents on a wide range of the most efficient ones."

"So you did business with him on a regular basis?"

"Not at all. I left ordering supplies to Gideon. I can't be bothered to waste my time on trivial things," he said indignantly, puffing himself up in self-importance.

"But you wasted your time to go pick him up," Cassie pointed out. "You knew him well enough to bail him out."

"Gideon insisted. He said the mix-up was his fault, so we had to stop what we were doing and rush to the rescue." Charlie's voice left no question what he had felt about the interruption. "It was damned inconsiderate, if you ask me. We were right in the middle of an experiment."

"Wouldn't you have needed John's whatever-it-was to finish your experiment?"

"What? Oh, no," he clarified, "our work didn't call for amphiphilic polymers. We were concentrating on agricultural terra-forming - reshaping environmental conditions of a geographic location into an area more conducive for recreational pursuits." At Cassie's frown, he explained further. "Turning marshland into prime real estate for amusement parks. It had the potential to be truly groundbreaking, but Gideon decided we would be better off focusing on a less commercial endeavor."

"If you weren't using John's whatchamacallits for your experiments, why did Gideon bail him out? Why did he blame himself for John getting arrested?" Cassie was thinking out loud, but to her surprise, Charles volunteered an answer.

"I suppose it was for his pet project."

"Hang on a second," Cassie said, her eyes narrowing in anger as she realized Charlie had just admitted he had lied to her. "You said Gideon wasn't working on anything in particular before he died. You said he was between projects."

"He was." Throughout the course of their conversation, his complexion had completely restored itself to its natural hue, but now it bleached even further as he realized he had made a potentially fatal mistake. "He did have some crazy theory he was playing around with, but that was years ago. I'm sure he'd given up on it. He must have."

Cassie's smile was feral. "I want you to tell me

everything about it. Don't leave out a single detail. And remember," she said with relish, "I won't hesitate to bring out the big guns if I think you're holding out on me... I know where they keep the cod liver oil and brussel sprouts."

Charlie gulped, his Adam's apple bobbing nervously up and down. "It was something to do with the cataclysm. He wanted to find a way to control the changes people underwent – to be able to consciously manipulate them."

Holy shit. Designer transformations?

Now that was something worth coming back from the dead for.

Chapter Eleven

Cassie stared out her bedroom window. The sun was pale and anemic, but it was still relatively high in the sky. She had plenty of time to get to the barn and back before it got dark.

She went over the contents of her oversized bag, making sure she had everything she would need. Taser, machete, blowtorch with a fully reloaded fuel supply...

Gideon's invention was the key to this whole thing. She was sure of it. It was what brought him back to life; maybe why he was killed in the first place. After all, who could pass up the opportunity to control the Cataclysm?

The way it stood now, transformations were unpredictable. Sure, magic searched out a person's inner beliefs, but how many people actively chose what they believed in? Most just went along with what they had learned as children, following more from habit than true conviction. Besides, just because you believed in something didn't mean you wanted to become it.

Cassie believed in bad-hair days. That didn't mean she wanted to have a perpetual one.

Being able to choose what you became meant you could literally become anything you wanted to be. It had the potential to truly reshape the world.

And like all earth-shattering ideas, if the wrong person got hold of it, all hell would break loose.

Cassie had to find Gideon and his project and make sure that didn't happen.

She had a pretty good idea where it was. Strange noises, odd lights, and a strong chemical odor - all classic signs of paranormal activity. What better way to cover up a secret lab than to put it in a place already known for bizarre occurrences?

The barn was the logical place to look, so that's where she would head.

There was a loud knock on the door. She opened it to find David, looking heart-wrenchingly attractive in dark blue jeans and a heavy wool sweater. He barged into the room without waiting for her to invite him. "I want to talk to you."

"I don't think there's anything we need to say." Cassie tried to ignore the way her skin felt like it had come into contact with a live wire as he brushed by her. "Unless you've come to confess something…"

Barely looking at her, he started talking, spitting the words out at a break-neck pace. "I've been thinking about what happened at the cottage." Tugging at the ring on his right hand, he worked it restlessly with his fingers. "I've thought about it a lot, and I realized there were a few things I needed to explain…"

He trailed off as he noticed the bag on the floor.

His gaze dropped to the belt around her waist, loaded with her hunting knives. "Are you going somewhere?"

"I'd rather not say. You have your secrets, I have mine."

His expression clouded over. "I thought we went over this before. It's not safe for you to go out by yourself." A muscle in his jaw tightened in an angry tic. "I'll take you wherever you need to go."

She snorted. "And interfere with my investigation? Not likely. I'll be fine on my own."

She always was.

David advanced on her with a dangerous look in his eyes. "You will *not* go out by yourself. Period." He rested his hands on her shoulders, gently but firmly preventing her from running away.

This close to him, Cassie could feel every nerve in her body leap to life, sizzling with the need to expand the contact. She licked her lips, fighting the urge to lick his instead. "And you're going to stop me how?" She had meant the question as an insult, but she knew the huskiness in her voice wasn't entirely due to anger.

Her hope David wouldn't realize that was shattered when he moved even closer, his eyes dilated so wide she felt she could drown in them.

"Don't mistake politeness for being a pushover," he said, his own voice deepening to a raspy growl. "I know you have a job to do, and even if I don't agree it's necessary, I won't try to stop you, but if you don't take the necessary precautions, I will hound your every move." His fingers started to move back and forth on her shoulder, tracing the line of her collarbone. "You won't be able to take a step without me beside you."

"Just try it." Unbidden, her hands slipped to his waist, settling on the broad, hard plane of his stomach. "I'll have you hog-tied and begging for mercy before you know what hit you."

He groaned, a sound made up of equal parts anger and desire. "Cassie..."

"David," she challenged, hearing the longing in her own voice. "What are you gonna do to stop me?"

He tugged her to him, kissing her with an intensity she hadn't known he was capable of. His hands seemed to be everywhere, running across her back and skimming over her ass as if he were trying to memorize every inch of her.

She knew the feeling. Her own hands were busy caressing him, stroking his arms, his chest, anywhere and everywhere she could reach. As they staggered towards the bed, Cassie fumbled with her belt, managing to drop it to the floor seconds before they toppled onto the thick mattress.

So much better.

Now she could reach more, could feel the muscles straining in his legs as she wrapped hers around them. She wrenched off his shirt so that she could feel his bare flesh under her hands and mouth. He was perfectly sculpted, his torso a mass of rippling muscles under firm, resilient skin. Skin that tasted better than champagne... that tasted like pure hot, delicious man.

Unwilling to let her have all the fun, David

pushed the jacket off her shoulders, baring her thin silk chemise. Judging from the wolfish smile he gave her, it met with his full approval. He rolled her over onto her back and pinned her lightly under his weight, using his teeth to urge the silk higher.

As the chemise rose up, his smile grew more dangerous.

Cassie threw her head back in delight, her back arching in an effort to bring him closer. The warmth of his breath combined with the feel of his teeth grazing her skin was painfully erotic, creating a desperate pull all through her body.

Her legs wrapped around his hips, pressing him to her. "David..." she moaned.

Heat was building everywhere, scorching her with fiery tendrils and threatening to consume them both until they were nothing more than ashes on the wind. Sinking her fingers into his shoulders, she urged the flames higher, knowing there was no way she'd rather go.

Desperate to taste him, to prove she affected him the same way he did her, she flipped them over and pinned him to the mattress. Straddling his chest, she stared in wonder at the sight in front of her. His chest was heaving beneath her legs, shuddering with each deep, uneven breath he took. His hands were trembling as they lifted to lie reverently on her hips. And his eyes...

Oh, God. His eyes...

They were locked onto her, searing her with their intensity. Unwilling to think about what the look meant, she dropped her head and claimed his mouth in a passionate kiss.

There was no telling where one began and the other ended... no thoughts of who was the aggressor and who was submitting... the two melded into one, switching back and forth between giving and taking as effortlessly as if it was part of their genes. Beads of sweat formed on the back of Cassie's neck as her temperature rose. It felt as if she were turning into molten steel; all she wanted to do was pour herself over David, surrounding him until he was encased within her, breathing the same air and sharing the same heartbeat.

Her palms moved urgently over his chest, trailing a path from a point just above his heart to the top of his jeans. His hips bucked underneath her and he let out a pleading moan.

She deftly undid the button and began to ease his zipper down.

His hands slid from her hair, pushing gently on her shoulders as he struggled to sit up and shuck his clothes the rest of the way off. When he was done, he turned to her. Lifting his hand to caress her cheek, his eyes darkened with passion, burning with a fierce light that rocked her to her core.

"God, Cass... you're driving me crazy," he whispered in ragged breaths stolen between urgent, hungry kisses. "I can't think straight when you're around."

The feeling was mutual. She would have told him so, but she was incapable of coherent thought.

His mouth moved to graze along her throat, trailing a line of fire along it. "You're everything I've ever wanted. Never want to let you go."

It was little more than a whisper, but it stopped her cold.

Sooner or later, he *would* let her go - but not before breaking her heart.

Better sooner than later.

"Stop." Her voice was harsh and ragged – barely recognizable, even to her own ears. "I can't... We can't do this."

Instantly, he stilled, dropping his hands to the side.

She scrambled off the bed, grabbing her top off the floor and pulling it on. "This is a mistake. You should go now." She kept her back to him, facing the door, but she could hear the rustle of clothes being thrown on and zipped up. When she turned around, he was sitting on the bed. His hands were shaking, and his shoulder muscles were tight knots under his skin.

She wanted to reach out and touch him, to massage the tension from his shoulders and kiss the worry lines from his forehead.

Lines she had put there.

"I'm sorry." His words were so quiet she could barely hear them. "I shouldn't have let myself get carried away."

"Don't," she snapped. "Don't apologize." She was the one who had screwed up. It was her fault. Her and her damned – and damning – curse. "You didn't do anything wrong."

She could tell he didn't believe it. It was in the way he sat, angled away from her and refusing to meet her gaze. She couldn't stand seeing him that way. She needed to tell him, to explain why she couldn't let him get close. "Earlier, you said you wanted to talk. I think that might be a good idea."

For a minute, he was silent, then he shook his head as if to clear it. "I'm sorry. I can't." He stood up, avoiding her gaze. "Not now."

He walked to the door, stopping when he reached it, with his hand on the knob. "I know I don't have the right to ask you for anything, but please don't leave the house without an escort." His voice was raspy with strain. "Please just take someone along."

She watched his hand tighten on the door as he waited for her answer, his knuckles turning white.

"Alright." It was hard speaking over the hard lump wedged in her throat. "I promise."

He nodded, never turning around. "Thank you."

The door closed behind him.

Chapter Twelve

Besides the appearance of zombies, werewolves, and other supernatural creatures, there were other less easily apparent side effects of the Cataclysm, such as the resurrection of Murphy's Law.

*Because, let's face it, deep down **everyone** believes that anything that can go wrong will usually do so, and almost invariably at the worst possible time.*

***

Cassie would keep her promise to David. She couldn't give him much, but she could give him that.

She found Striker in the east wing of the house, busy going over some security arrangements with the house staff. The bandage around his head was gone, replaced by a small plaster that was barely noticeable. He was obviously in his element, a warrior king issuing orders to his devoted followers. She watched as he gave instructions to each of the employees.

"Gideon has gotten inside the house at least once that we know of. He'll probably try again, so we have to be ready. If you do see him, do not let him into the house, but do not hurt him unless your life is in immediate danger. I repeat, do not hurt him. He is a MacDuff, and as such, he is still your employer."

She had to admit, his orders were logical, practical, and efficient.

They were also almost totally useless.

There was no reason to prevent Gideon from entering the house. If anything, they should be encouraging it. His family would be delighted if he walked in through the front door. So would Cassie. It would make her job that much easier.

Unfortunately, Gideon had chosen to stay away. He had, to all intents and purposes, cut himself off from his family, and in the time Cassie had been there, he hadn't tried to make any contact with them. He had snuck into the house once, but he hadn't tried to talk to anyone. Instead, he had been going through paperwork.

He's looking for something, and the quickest way to figure out his intentions is to let him find it.

If he was looking for something to do with his invention, she'd let him come back to claim it, and then after she'd helped him regain his peace, she could make sure his creation got to the proper authorities.

Or better yet… I could find it first.

That's why she was going to explore the barn mentioned in the police reports.

She waited until Striker wrapped up his meeting before stepping into his view.

A knowing smile spread over his face. "Back for more, huh?" His feet spread apart, his arms on his hips in a cocky pose. "I knew you wouldn't be able to stay away."

Huh. She had thought she'd made it pretty clear she wasn't interested in him, but apparently his head injury had left him a little muddled.

She'd have to make it a little clearer.

"I'm not looking for a personal relationship, Striker. Strictly business, remember?"

"Works for me." He cocked his head to the side. "You got any news yet?"

Glad to see he wasn't hurt by her lack of interest, she got straight to the point. "Some. You said you wanted to help with Gideon's case. I've got a lead, if you're still interested."

Striker's body stilled like Cerberus catching the scent of a lost soul. "I'm interested. Tell me what you've got."

"Let me show you instead."

***

The barn looked exactly like what you'd expect from a haunted building. It had weathered gray wood, with patches of peeling red paint in the few places the wind hadn't managed to strip totally. An ill-fitted shutter banged noisily against a badly cutout window frame high above, and the wind was whistling through gaps in the planks of the wall, creating a high pitch keening that could make the hairs on the back of your neck stand straight up.

Cassie motioned for Striker to cover her back.

"Stay behind me. I want to see if anyone's home before we go barging in."

"We don't have time to waste." Ignoring her instructions, he surged in front of her and burst through the door.

Looks like someone needs to work on his impulse control. "I *was* planning on knocking first. Someone lives here, you know."

"Just a ghost." Looking around, he proceeded to survey their surroundings, gun in hand.

Just a ghost? Obviously, Striker didn't realize it never paid to piss the supernatural off. They could get pretty obsessive in their revenge. Cassie knew of one specter who had filed eighty-three separate harassment and invasion of privacy charges against a paranormal investigator who wouldn't leave him alone.

Fortunately, she didn't see any pitchforks floating towards them, and there were no anguished howls of despair or mention of lawsuits echoing around their heads. "You're lucky you didn't make it mad."

"You want someone who's going to get the job done whatever the cost, I'm your guy. You want someone nice, look elsewhere."

He had a point. David wouldn't have broken the door. David would have knocked and waited for an answer.

And then held the door for her.

Striker was busy scouting the perimeter of the room, poking into rounded bales of hay. He pulled the tarp off a large pile that turned out to be a ride-on mower. "There probably aren't any ghosts here, anyway."

"Maybe." Cassie started looking for any trapdoors or hidden rooms. *Nothing.* "But it's still polite to check first."

Out of the corner of her eye, she noticed a ladder leading to a loft above. The ladder looked dilapidated, appearing to be unable to bear the weight of a small child, let alone a full-grown adult, but Cassie was willing to bet it was stronger than it looked. The rust was too evenly distributed, looking like it had been painted on by someone a little too fond of symmetry.

"I think I found something." She made her way to the ladder, testing the rungs by pulling on them with all her might. She was right; Their frail appearance was deceptive. They didn't budge an inch. "If I was trying to hide something, this is where I'd put it."

She started to climb. Striker hurried to follow, pushing at her in his haste to get to the top.

"Slow down, I'm almost there," she said.

He didn't listen, jostling her just as she threw her leg over the top rung and knocking her to the floor of the loft.

On the good side, she landed in a loose pile of hay that broke her fall. On the bad side, Striker's eagerness caused him to trip as well, sending him sprawling on top of her. The impact knocked the breath out of her, her eyes widening in shock.

Taking advantage of having Cassie pinned underneath him, Striker smirked down at her.

"You sure I can't change your mind about not mixing business with pleasure? We fit pretty well together."

She opened her mouth to give him an emphatic "no" when he swooped in for the kill.

Technically, it wasn't a bad kiss. His style wasn't hideous, and in the past, she might have gone for it.

But he wasn't David.

"Knock it off." She pushed at his chest with both hands, giving herself room to move her head away. As she did, she saw something shining from the middle of a lopsided stack of hay. With a shove, she pushed him the rest of the way off. "Look."

Rushing to the hay pile, she brushed the top layer off, revealing an assortment of glass beakers and flasks that had been haphazardly covered up. Digging further, she found rubber tubing and a Bunsen burner.

"Got you." She crouched down, examining the area closely. "See these streaks?" She pointed to a stretch of darkened wood, flecked with a crusty reddish-orange substance. "Those are residual chemical burns. I'm willing to bet Gideon was here."

She scraped some of the residue into a glass container, sealing it off before dropping it in her bag. "Let's see what else he left behind." She picked up a beaker for further examination, her eyes watering at the acrid scent coming from the dried powder left in its base.

"Is that it? Is that what Gideon was working

on?" Striker asked, crowding over her shoulder.

"Part of it, anyway."

"Do you know what it was?"

"I think so." She picked up another flask, this one with a pleasant fruity scent. "Charlie told me he was working on a way to control the kind of transformations people go through."

"Charlie, huh?" Striker grunted. "I never thought to find out if that weasel knew anything. So Gideon found a way to do it? Pretty impressive. No wonder he figured I wouldn't understand what he was doing."

"I can't tell if he found a way or not. My guess is he was close to completion when he was killed, so he came back to finish it. Maybe he even thinks he can bring himself back to fully human with it." She passed the flask to Striker, giving him the chance to examine it for himself. "There's not enough here to say, but I can get a better idea of what he was doing if we figure out what kind of chemicals he was using."

He handed the flask back to her. "How do we do that?"

"By having what's in these beakers analyzed."

"Sounds like a plan." He started to sift through the hay, looking for anything she might have missed.

They worked silently, each focused on their task and each searching different parts of the loft. It went on that way for several minutes, until the sound of breaking glass caused Cassie to stop what she was doing. "Careful, we can't afford to lose any of this."

Striker shook his head. "It wasn't me. I thought

it was you."

Another crash sounded, louder than the one before, and this time Cassie could tell it was coming from below.

"Shit. We've got company. Pack everything up quickly." She started randomly throwing things in her bag; she'd sort them later.

A blood-curdling wail came out of nowhere, coupled with more breaking glass.

"What the hell is that?" Striker asked, covering his ears. A cold wind had begun to blow through the barn, pulling at her bag and stirring the loose hay around, making it difficult to see.

"I think the owner of the house is back, and he doesn't sound happy."

"Here, I'll take that. You get downstairs and out of here." Striker grabbed the bag from out of her hands, shoving her towards the ladder. "Go," he yelled when she hesitated, "I'll deal with the ghoulie."

She shimmied down the ladder. "I'm down, now it's your turn. Come on," she screamed over the noise swirling around them.

His legs appeared over the edge as he grabbed the top rung. "Don't wait for me, make a run for it." The wind was picking up, creating a vortex that was threatening to pull him off the ladder. If he fell the wrong way, he was going to land on the bag full of glass.

Not wanting him to injure himself, she yelled, 'Throw my bag down!"

"What?" He was trying to descend, but his foot

kept slipping off the rung, pushed by currents of air.

"Drop the bag!"

It was no use. He couldn't hear her.

She ran towards the open doorway, intent on getting help. She had a magical emergency kit back at the car; she could conjure up something to exorcise the ghost temporarily. "Hang on, I'll be right back."

From behind her, a roar thundered, full of anger.

"I'm sorry, we'll pay to have the door repaired." She sprinted towards the outside.

A hand on her wrist stopped her. A very old, very wrinkled, and very *dead* hand.

She turned to look, knowing what she was going to see, but wishing she was wrong anyway.

She wasn't. The zombie was old and desiccated as the ones that had attacked her and Striker before, but this one had only one arm, and an extremely pissed off expression on the gnarled remains of its face.

It roared again, groaning incoherently as it tried to get close enough to bite her.

She felt bad about what she was going to do, but it had left her no choice. She needed to take care of it as quickly as possible so she could concentrate on helping Striker.

Taking a hunting knife from her belt, she slashed out. The arm restraining her quickly fell away, both from her and the zombie it had previously been attached to.

It should have been enough to stop him, but

the zombie kept on coming. Its mouth opened wide, revealing a gaping maw of bad oral hygiene. By the looks of it, its teeth had been long gone even before it had died and been resurrected.

What's it trying to do – gum me to death?

Behind her, Striker screamed in fury. He was clinging to the ladder as the wind continued to pummel him, with only one hand still gripping the rung in a losing attempt to keep from falling. The other arm flailed madly as he tried to regain his balance.

"Hold on," Cassie yelled, kicking out at the zombie advancing towards her. "I'm almost done here." Her heel sunk into the undead's papery flesh, sending a cloud of dust gusting up into the swirling air. The heel stuck in his body, so she pulled her foot back sans shoe.

Hopping on her other leg so as not to cause a run in her silk stockings, she carved a circular pattern into the zombie's chest with her knife.

The circle of desiccated flesh fell towards the ground, releasing the shoe into Cassie's waiting hand.

"That's better," she said, putting it on. "Now where were we?" She smiled at the zombie, using her most charming 'I am not here to kill you unless you really annoy me' look. "Are you sure you wouldn't rather talk about this? I'm a good listener."

The zombie roared again, a wordless groan of incoherent rage as it charged in a headlong rush.

"Come on now, you're not even trying," she said, stepping aside.

It flew by her, its momentum causing it to crash into the bottom of the ladder Striker was dangling from. Or to be more accurate, the ladder Striker *had* been dangling from.

Cassie grimaced as Striker lost his holding. "Sorry about that." At least he had a soft landing. The zombie cushioned his fall like an oddly shaped and entirely decrepit beanbag. She ran to him, helping him up and away from the zombie. "You okay?"

His eyes were unfocused and they rolled up into the back of his head as he collapsed to the floor.

Behind them, the zombie was attempting to rise, rolling around trying to find some way to push himself up. Cassie watched it struggle, but all it managed to do was spin itself around in a circle.

"Can I help you with that?" she asked politely. Before it could answer, a huge shriek reverberated through the barn, shaking the walls and momentarily distracting her. "Excuse me," she said, raising her voice, "can you keep it down? I'm trying to have a conversation here."

In response, the wind picked up, this time joined by the sound of clanking chains and unearthly screams.

"Look, I said I'm sorry for the door, and I've promised to pay for a new one. I'll even buy one that's two upgrades above what you have now." Crossing her arms, her foot began to tap impatiently. "But that goes out the window if you're not going to be reasonable about this whole thing."

The wind died suddenly,

"That's more like it. Now how about a little help?" She pointed towards the helpless creature on the floor and an unseen force assisted it to its feet and held it in place.

"Thank you." A wave of grudging welcome pulsed through the room.

"So," Cassie said, addressing the zombie with the little patience she had left, "Let's chat."

***

Cassie knelt by the side of the grave and dusted her hands off. Questioning the zombie had proved spectacularly unhelpful. It hadn't said anything to her – but then it was hard to talk when you didn't have a tongue. She had managed to get some information just from observing him up close, but in all, the barn's ghost had proved more useful, moving the hay aside in areas where more lab equipment had been hidden.

Not willing to let the zombie suffer more than it already was, she had dispatched it as painlessly as she could , brought its remains to the sand pit behind the barn. After making sure the flames in the pit were completely out, she stood up and walked to the car.

Striker sat in the passenger's side with the safety belt drawn tightly around him to keep him from falling over. His head lolled listlessly to one side, but the soft snores coming from him were deep and even.

She slid into the driver's seat, taking a last

glance of the sand pit in the rear-view mirror. The smoke had already faded away, leaving no sign as to what had happened there.

Cassie started the engine. Pushing the speed of the car to its full extent, she raced through the winding, narrow roads, oblivious to both the scenery surrounding her and the unconscious man beside her.

Something was bothering her, nagging at her thoughts like an insistent little landshark nibbling on sunbathers' toes. She was close, but the pieces weren't fitting the way they should. Gideon had definitely used the barn for his experiments, but from the little the ghost had been able to communicate, he hadn't been there for months. If the experiment was the reason he had come back, why wouldn't he have come to check on it since his re-animation?

And then there was the zombie she had just dispatched. Someone had obviously been controlling it and the other zombies she had encountered, but who?

And why?

Her mind sorted through everything she had learned so far, sifting the relevant from the trivial until she could find a plausible explanation, but she felt like she was missing the critical information that would snap everything into focus.

She couldn't figure out what it was, though, and by the time she neared the castle, the sun was setting, hiding the countryside as effectively as the secrets she was trying to uncover were being hidden away. An orange-red glow hung over the tops of the trees beyond the front gates, giving it a sullen, foreboding look.

Which is entirely appropriate, considering the personality of the woods' guardian.

Cassie searched for signs of the dryad as she drove through the path that opened up before her. She knew Nim was out there somewhere, lying in wait to spring out on Cassie when she least expected it, and, in general, being as much of a nuisance as humanly possible.

Or nymphly possible, as the case may be.

Maybe the dryad knew something. Gideon had run to the woods the first time Cassie had seen him. Nim might be able to tell Cassie where he had been going.

Nestled in the dashboard's cup holder, her phone began to buzz, hopping around like a deranged Irish Riverdancer.

"What?" she snapped as she answered it.

"Hello to you, too." Ash's voice was unusually perky, even for her.

"You're in a good mood. What's up?"

"I'm just back from a run. One of the gammas claimed a wolf would always beat a fox in a foot race."

The gammas were a group of weres that slavishly followed Ash's dad around. They were constantly jockeying for a higher position in their social hierarchy, and every so often one came up with the brilliant idea to try and improve his or her standing by taking on their leader's daughter.

"Would they?" Cassie asked with genuine

interest.

"Not if they pull a hamstring first. Which, I'm sad to say, she did. Four of them, to be exact." To her credit, Ash managed to keep ninety-nine percent of the gloating from her voice.

Cassie wouldn't have done nearly as well. "Nothing permanent, I hope?"

"She'll be fine in a week when the spell's effects wear off. Maybe by then she will have learned never, *ever* to piss a werefox off. Especially one who has access to her mother's magical supply box," Ash purred, her voice smug. "And speaking of Mom," she continued after an infinitesimal pause, "I explained your current situation to her and she's on board. In fact, she has some very interesting ideas."

Cassie stole a glance at Striker. Satisfied he wasn't in any condition to understand what she and Ash were talking about, she said, "Tell her not to bother."

"What happened?" Ashley growled, her voice filled with compassion and just the right amount of indignation. "Never mind; you can tell me when I get there. I'll show him what happens to anyone who messes with a member of my pack."

"Ash, don't." Having Ashley's support meant more than she could ever admit, but Cassie didn't want her friend to think badly of David. "It's not his fault."

"Don't you dare tell me it's yours. I won't believe it."

"It is." She was supposed to know better. She

was supposed to keep her distance. "I screwed up pretty badly." She didn't think she'd ever forget the look on his face when he fled from her room. The pain in his eyes had been unbearable. He hadn't even tried to hide it; his emotions had been laid bare in front of her, leaving him looking vulnerable and defenseless. "I'm pretty sure he hates me now.

"Are you sure of that? I can't imagine..." Static crackled over the receiver, distorting the rest of Ash's reply.

"Ash... are you there? I can't hear you.""

"... keep trying... people... mistakes..." the words faded in and out. "explain... things... work out..."

The phone clicked off, leaving Cassie alone with nothing but Ash's fractured words of comfort and the sound of Striker's deep, untroubled snores.

Chapter Thirteen

The sun was setting, turning the sky a breathtaking multitude of colors. Shades of burnt orange mixed with slashes of faded rose and molten gold. The champagne in her glass was a paler shade of gold, but it was no less perfect. Tiny bubbles rose to the surface of their Waterford crystal flute, mirroring the bubbling in her heart.

She couldn't remember ever being this happy.

Taking a sip of champagne and savoring the combination that the cool, smooth crystal and the effervescent liquid formed against her lips, she felt as if nothing in the world could possibly make this moment any sweeter.

She was proven wrong a moment later when David replaced the touch of the glass on her lips with his own warm mouth. He was more intoxicating than any champagne. He made her head spin in a glorious tilt-a-whirl running at full speed.

He tasted her mouth with his tongue, slipping past the seam of her lips and delving further into her secrets. As the kiss deepened, she was barely aware of the cool air growing more intense on her skin as he unbuttoned her top.

As he reached out to caress her bare flesh with gentle hands, a jolt of electricity shot through her. She grabbed at his shirt hungrily, longing to feel his skin next to hers, but the champagne glass in her hand prevented her from tearing his clothes off.

She blindly set the glass down beside her.

"Oh good." The voice came from somewhere behind David, the slurred words alerting Cassie to disaster even before she raised her head. "If you're not going to drink that, do you mind if I have it?"

What the hell did Charlie think he was doing interrupting them at a time like this? He was going to ruin everything. Not that David seemed to mind. He was still kissing her, nibbling the column of her throat in a slow, leisurely path down to her collarbone.

Cassie shivered at the sensation.

Maybe she could pretend Charlie wasn't there, too.

No such luck.

Charles sat down, making himself comfortable on the edge of the picnic blanket. "Never mind, I'll just help myself to the bottle." He helped himself to a gorgonzola-and-prosciutto-stuffed fig as well. "Ah, that's much better."

Okay... this was a little much. "David..."

"Yes, my love?" David drew back immediately; an adoring look on his face. "How can I make things more perfect for you? Can I rub your back? Buy you that sports car you've been wanting? Serenade you with Spanish long songs?" Not waiting for an answer, he turned his attention back to her neck.

"I'd go for the car if I were you," Charles volunteered after taking a long gulp from the champagne bottle. "Automobiles are always a good investment."

What the hell was going on? Nothing was making any sense anymore!

"Tell me about it," another voice chimed in, directly behind Cassie.

Striker held up his hands, tied by the curtain sash she had pulled from the window in his room. "How 'bout letting me go so we can get back to our unfinished business? Or at least shift over - you're hogging the blanket." He struggled to sit and was thrown off balance by the loss of his hands.

Charles tried to assist him, but all he managed to do was send Striker crashing into the picnic basket, spilling its contents in a jumbled mess.

"Sorry," Charles slurred, "my fault."

"So, what do you say, Cass?" Striker asked, edging closer to her until he was practically pushing her off the blanket and onto the grass. "Have you decided you want a real man yet?"

"Cassie's too smart for you. She deserves only the best." David protested between kisses. "Besides, you only want a one-night stand."

"Yeah, but if she doesn't have a problem with it, why should I?" Striker put his hands on Cassie's shoulders to pull her away from David. "At least I don't lie to her."

"Excuse me," Charles piped up, "we seem to be running out of champagne."

Cassie turned on him with exasperation. "Seriously? What the fuck is up with you?"

Charles drew himself up as tall as he could in his current inebriated position. "Haven't you figured it out yet?"

He lurched forward, his eyes closed and his lips puckered in anticipation.

"Get away from me," she managed to choke out, almost overwhelmed by the stench of alcohol rising off of him.

He had gone nuts. They had all gone nuts - including her. There was no other explanation.

"What is wrong with you people?" she asked, scrambling off the blanket before they could stop her. "I can't figure out what any of you want from me!"

She stood up, ready to make a break for it. Before she could, a hand clapped down on her shoulder.

"What about me?" Gideon asked, his clothes tattered and torn and his graying face showing signs of decomposition. "Have you figured out what I want yet?"

**

In a perfect world, the sun would be shining brightly and the birds would be singing softly as Cassie rose from her bed, her eyes bright and cheerful after a peaceful night's rest, her tousled hair falling softly and beautifully around her shoulders. Instead, she stuck her arm out of the covers, blindly searching for the phone she had thrown on the bedside table.

Alarm clock, half-empty bottle of top-of-the-line Scotch, bottle of aspirin.

She kept searching until she found what felt like her phone, then brought it under the covers and pulled Ash up from her contact list. As the connection went through, Cassie winced in pain. Instead of the standard ringtone or even a nice soothing chime, Ash had programmed her cell to play an irritatingly loud and cheerful version of Warren Zevon's Werewolves of London.

Cassie held the phone away from her ear until she heard her friend's voice come on the line.

"Hi, this is Ash. I'm either not at home or don't have opposable thumbs right now. Leave a message at the howl and I'll get back to you."

"Ash, you twisted vixen," Cassie growled, "where are you? You never called me back after we got disconnected last night. Call me as soon as you get this message, or any blood spilled will be your responsibility, not mine."

Late last night, lying in bed, Ash's words – garbled as they were – had echoed through Cassie's head, robbing her of sleep. Was Ash right? Should she keep trying? David had withheld information from her, but he'd been adamant he hadn't done it on purpose. She wanted to believe him, but it was almost impossible.

Even if he had been trustworthy before she met him, her curse wouldn't let him stay that way.

If she could just talk to him and explain why she

felt the way she did... why she was having such a hard time trusting him... It would be so much easier if she could only be positive he would never lie to her again.

Maybe she could be... if she used Gideon's invention.

Excitement shot through her like a thunderbolt straight from Mount Olympus.

What if it really did what it was supposed to? It would be the solution to all her problems.

She could use it to make sure David would never betray her.

It wouldn't be like she'd be changing him; she'd just be changing the effect the curse had on him. And it wouldn't help just her. She'd make sure it would help him, too. She could bring Gideon back to life. The invention was the solution to *everything*. She just had to find it.

But how?

She had sent the samples from the barn out to be tested, but there hadn't been enough of the compounds left for the lab to identify. To make matters worse, the hospital had said Sasha wasn't in any condition to receive visitors, so questioning her would have to wait.

There were still a few leads she could follow, though, even if they weren't as promising.

Someone was raising puppet zombies – the ones who had attacked her and Striker, the one who had shown up at the barn, and possibly the one who had attacked Sasha – and they had to be coming from somewhere.

So it was off to the local cemeteries.

After picking out an outfit appropriate for the occasion - form-fitting black leather pants, a matching leather bustier, and her favorite red stiletto boots, she packed her bag with all the items she might need. Once that was done, she asked one of the servants who seemed to perpetually haunt the halls to deliver a message, and then headed downstairs to wait for a reply.

She avoided the breakfast salon, not wanting to run the risk of running into David, heading to the kitchen instead. The cook was nice enough to let her grab one of the pre-assembled yogurt parfaits stored in the fridge, and even offered to whip up a few sandwiches to take with her. Once she had stashed them in her bag, she made her way to the main living room and waited for her companion for the day.

It didn't take long for him to arrive.

"Good morning!" Charlie's voice boomed as he rushed into the living room, as loud and obnoxious as the outfit he was wearing. Dressed in an absurdly inappropriate ensemble made up of a bright orange hunting vest over a tweed jacket and pants, he looked like a cross between Sherlock Holmes and Elmer Fudd. "I was delighted to receive your message. I must say, the opportunity to explore a possible zombie infestation site with you has left me positively exhilarated."

He doesn't look exhilarated. He looks obnoxious. And irritating.

Why the hell had she agreed to let him

accompany her on her investigation to the graveyards again?

Because I promised David I wouldn't go anywhere alone, that's why, and I'm going to keep that promise if it kills me. Or Charlie.

Preferably Charlie.

"I'm thrilled you reconsidered," he nattered on. "Not surprised, of course. I knew you would come to realize how much of an asset I could be. I may not have your practical experience, but my theoretical knowledge will undoubtedly prove invaluable, eh, Cassandra? I may call you Cassandra, mayn't I?"

Cassie bit the inside of her cheek and reminded herself that, as bitter a pill as it was to swallow, she needed the Englishman. As irritating as he was, he knew the area, and everyone else was unavailable. She would have taken Striker, but he was still feeling the aftereffects of their outing to the barn.

She supposed she could have conscripted one of MacDuff's other security guards to help her, but she didn't want to do anything to undermine Striker's authority. It's not like she needed hired muscle, anyway. She doubted they would run into any trouble, but if they did, she'd be able to handle it by herself.

"Oh, I say," Charlie exclaimed, digging through the bag she'd set down on an end table. "You've packed a picnic lunch. Splendid."

She grabbed the bag away from him. "Stay out of there."

"Of course, of course. But I couldn't help noticing your proliferation of weapons. Perhaps I should bring something as well? I can run up to my room to grab my fencing foil."

Cassie gritted her teeth. "That won't be necessary," she said, twisting her lips into what she hoped looked like a smile and not the snarl she really wanted to present.

"Are you sure? It won't take any time at all, and I'm quite good. I took fourth place in the World University games." He started to the door, moving eagerly.

"Charlie, stop!"

He halted. "Yes?"

"You're not going to need it, I promise."

"Are you sure?"

"Positive. This isn't a hunting trip."

"It's not?"

"No. Think of it more as research. You should know all about that, right?"

"I see. Research." His eyes dropped to her bag. "In a graveyard. With a picnic lunch."

"No reason we should starve ourselves doing it." *God, it's like explaining things to a two-year-old.* "Let's just go enjoy the fresh air and see if we can figure anything out, okay?"

His expression cleared with sudden comprehension. "Oh. Of course. I hadn't realized." He looked down at his vest. "I would have dressed differently if I had known..."

Thank God. She'd finally gotten through to him. "Don't worry about it. You look fine."

"As do you. Quite fetching."

Maybe it won't be so bad having him along.

"You have quite good taste... for an American, anyway."

Then again, maybe it will be.

Chapter Fourteen

Lawyers hit the big time with the Cataclysm.

Hundreds of new regulations were debated, weighing the individual rights of new species versus the collective good of human society as a whole. After long, painstaking, (and expensive) arguments from lawyers on both sides, a compromise was ultimately reached that managed to satisfy neither camp.

The lawyers themselves were ecstatic, as they now had a whole new field of policies to screw up.

*About the only consistently good things to come out of the new regulations was the law that mandated all newly manufactured coffins must come equipped with an emergency exit beacon and a copy of the educational brochure, "**So You're a Zombie Now – Your Rights and Obligations in Three Easy to Understand Steps**".*

> ***Step 1*** *Do not eat anyone. Eating people will be considered anti-social behavior and will result in full prosecution by the relevant authorities.*

> ***Step 2*** *Please be courteous and pick up any stray body parts that may fall off of you. Failure to comply will result in full prosecution by*

the relevant authorities. Give a hoot, don't pollute.

Step 3 *Upon reanimating, each formerly dead entity (hereafter to be referenced as the "undead applicant") shall be required to fill out four copies of referendums **A125**, **316-A** and **316-B**, document **LLR-1262**, and a **Request for Continuation of Post-Existence(revised)**. Upon completion of these forms, the undead applicant shall then be required to file one copy of the form at each of the following locations: the municipal courthouse where the undead applicant was currently residing at the time of his/her/its termination of life, the census office listed as the official birthplace of the undead applicant, the Federal Proprietary Paraspecies Claims Bureau (**FPPCB**), and the Department of Public Welfare (**DPW**), currently located in Lwengo, Uganda.*

Failure to comply within 24 hours of reanimation will constitute a breach of contract and will result in full prosecution by the relevant authorities, leading up to and including an immediate reclamation of all rights to continued existence.

No one could say they hadn't been warned.

***

By the time they hit the third cemetery, Cassie was really, really hoping to find a few open graves. If she did, she could push Charlie in one and no one would be the wiser.

Unfortunately, the graves here were all in pristine condition. If she wanted to bury him six feet under, she was going to have to dig first. Since she was particularly fond of her nails today - a scarlet wrap with tips a half-shade darker - he was safe.

For now, anyway.

"I could have told you we wouldn't find anything here," he droned on as they finished their tour of the eastern branch of the cemetery. Nothing new about that - he hadn't shut up since leaving the house. "Most of the graves here are pre-cataclysm."

"I know." It was her main reason for coming here first. "The zombies I saw were all old." She had gone over this already. Several times. She was beginning to think he was either going deaf or getting senile.

"Yes, but they couldn't be this old. At the normal rate of decomposition for human bodies, we'd be lucky to find anything more than skeletons here." He bent down, brushing some dirt of a tombstone to reveal the epitaph. "See - date of death, 1979. Positively ancient."

Cassie read the rest of the inscription. "Stranger tread this ground with gravity, Dentist Brown is filling his last cavity." Apparently, dentist Brown was filling it peacefully; the soil was packed tightly and blanketed with a dense covering of hearty green grass.

"A sad display of sophomoric humor," Charlie declared, puffing up with indignation. "Last words should be profound... meaningful."

"Are you sure you don't want a drink?" She wouldn't have thought it possible, but Charlie was even more annoying when he wasn't drinking. At least when he was drunk, he was good for a laugh.

She didn't know why he had chosen to go cold turkey, but she wanted it to stop.

"Take, for example, the immortal words of Robert Louis Stevenson," he continued, his voice taking on a rich sonorous cadence. "Under the wide and starry sky, dig the grave and let me lie. Glad did I live and gladly die, and I laid me down with a will. This be the verse you grave for me: Here he lies where he longed to be. Home is the sailor, home from the sea, And the hunter home from the hill." As he drew to a close, he took a deep bow.

"Uh-huh. Does that even rhyme?" Without looking to see if he was following, Cassie moved on to the next section of the cemetery. They were moving into the more recent additions, people who had been buried within the last ten years. "Besides, what's wrong with a little humor? People are already depressed when they come here. Why not try to cheer them up a little?"

"But what about leaving a legacy?" he asked, picking his way gingerly over the graves as he trailed behind her. "Shouldn't we strive to provide inspiration and hope for the people we've left behind?"

"If you didn't do it while you were alive, what do you think you're going to accomplish when you're dead? Nope, I think I'll stick to the funny ones." She stopped to look around, disappointed as she realized that there were no open graves here, either.

Damn, she really could have gone for a good fight right about now.

Charlie, not noticing she had stopped, stumbled into her, knocking his glasses off and stepping on her feet. Cassie brightened. If he had left a scuffmark on her stiletto boots, she might get that fight after all.

"Terribly sorry." He muttered quickly, stooping to pick up his glasses and polish them on his shirt. Without them, his pale blue eyes seemed more focused, less vague.

Or maybe it was just that he was sober.

"Forget about it," she told him gruffly. "Just don't do it again."

He cleared his throat, obviously preparing to launch into another long-winded speech.

Great. That was the last thing she wanted to hear.

"You are a truly remarkable woman, Ms. Jones."

"Yeah, right."

"I mean it, truly. And I'd like to offer my most sincere apologies to you. I'm afraid I haven't been at my best in our previous encounters. I fear I allowed myself to become slightly inebriated."

"You mean you were shit-faced drunk?" She wouldn't hold that against him. She'd been known to overindulge once or twice herself. "Yeah, so what about it?"

"I believe I may have given you the wrong impression of me. With your permission, I would like to attempt to correct that."

In her new-found spirit of forgiveness, she was willing to cut him some slack. She patted him on the shoulder. "Sure, no problem."

He looked down at her hand, his face turning an alarming shade of red.

Shit. She hoped he wasn't having a heart attack or anything. She looked for a bench for him to sit down on, only to be interrupted when he spoke again.

"You can't comprehend how happy I am to hear you say that." Before she knew what he was doing, he grabbed her in a passionate embrace. "I'll do everything I can to make you happy, Cassandra." He pressed his mouth to hers, silencing any protests she might have before she could voice them.

Wow. Cassie's head began to spin as she realized she was sort of enjoying the kiss. *Not bad for a geezer.*

It was surprisingly good. Just enough pressure, not too much tongue. And he tasted like cinnamon and cloves, with just a hint of whiskey.

Guess he hadn't gone cold turkey after all.

She let it go on for longer than she should, stopping only when she felt his hands starting to slip down her back to rest on the upper curve of her ass.

"Whoa, stop right there, Charlie," she said, pulling back. "An apology is one thing, but let's not get carried away."

"You're right; I'm doing this entirely out of

order. I haven't let you know my intentions yet."

"Intentions? You've got intentions?"

"I will admit it hadn't occurred to me until you invited me on this date…"

"Date? What date? This isn't a date!"

"… and I know I haven't given you the best examples of my suitability, but I can assure you, I am fully capable of conducting myself in a most amorous manner. A manner which I believe you would find a certain pleasure in, if I might be so bold to add."

She'd give him that, if the kiss was any example of what he was capable of.

"You and I would make a magnificent couple. Your sense of courage and your obvious physical prowess, my superior intellect and keen sense of scientific principles – just think of the team we would make. Think of the children we would create."

"Children?!"

"Of course we'll have children. As many as you like, although I must say I would prefer no more than three." His gaze dropped from her eyes to her chest with a look of politely restrained lust. "However, I'm entirely willing to negotiate that number, if it's important to you." Suddenly, he sank down on one knee. Placing one hand over his heart and holding the other one out to her, he asked, "Cassandra, would you do me the great honor of becoming my wife?"

What?

WHAT?!

"Charlie, what the hell are you talking about? I can't marry you!"

"I know I'm a few years older than you, but what does that signify? I'm still in my physical prime, and did I mention my inventions have made me inordinately wealthy?" His blue eyes gleamed, assured of her eventual compliance.

"I am not going to marry you." *Just how wealthy was inordinately wealthy?* "I have absolutely no desire to marry you."

"Ah." He paused, considering her response. "We'll live together then. You're right; marriage is an archaic institution, what need have we for a legal piece of paper to solemnize our union?"

"Charlie, I want you to listen very carefully to me. We are not getting married, we are not living together, we are not doing *anything* together. There will be absolutely, positively no repeat of what just happened between us. Do I make myself perfectly clear?"

Charles stared up at her, a dawning look of horror on his face.

"Aw, now, don't take it so hard. You're not a bad guy," she said, stretching the truth a little for diplomacy's sake, "and I'll admit you've got one hell of a technique, but it just wouldn't work between us." She looked to see how he was taking it.

It wasn't well. His face was a mottled purple, his mouth opening and closing in disbelief. "ZZ...zzz..."

Oh shit, he really was having a heart attack. What was the first aid for that again? She was almost sure it was something to do with elevating the feet. Or was she supposed to clear his windpipe first? She knelt down beside him, reaching for his chin to make sure he hadn't swallowed his tongue.

"Zombie!" He managed to yell; his eyes focused on a spot over Cassie's shoulder.

With a sense of resignation, Cassie turned to look.Sure enough, the ground of the grave closest to her was churning, the grass breaking away and falling to the side as bottom soil rose to the top in a frenzied maelstrom.

Looking over her shoulder, she saw Charles slide the rest of the way into incoherence, passing out in a boneless heap. "Right, I'll take care of this, you wait here," she told his unconscious figure.

Fingers started to claw their way into the open air, followed by a tattered sleeve on an equally tattered arm.

Cassie sighed. "Can you hurry it up a little? I'm right in the middle of something here." Tired of waiting, she walked to the grave and used her hands to clear away soil.

Within moments, the zombie erupted, bursting out of the now open pit with an agonized groan.

"Yeah, yeah. I take it you've read the pamphlet?" She asked as he advanced on her, roaring in incoherent rage. "Can I assume you don't have any plans on filling out the necessary paperwork?"

The zombie's only reaction was to lurch menacingly towards her, drool dripping down the side of its partially decayed face.

"Ok, but don't say I didn't give you a chance." With the formalities out of the way, she sprung towards it and swept its legs out from beneath it in a low tackle. She could feel its arms pounding on her back as it tried to claw her off, but she held on, rolling it back towards its grave.

A few feet away, it managed to dig its heels in, stopping their progress.

"My, you're a feisty one, aren't you... Reginald?" she said after consulting his tombstone. "I'd feel bad about this if you weren't a puppet. But I can't let your master keep making more of you guys, so – back you go."

She wrapped his head in her arms and trapping him in a nuclear headlock she had picked up from watching professional wrestling threw him into the remains of his splintered coffin.

Jumping in after him, she threw herself on top of him, using her weight to hold him down. Her hands clenched on his shoulders and her scarlet fingernails pressed into his flesh, pinning him to the ground so she could take control. He reached out to wrap his hands around her in an attempt to pull or shove her off, his legs frantically bucking an attempt to dislodge her any way possible.

She held on, her fingernails digging into his flesh as she kept him pinned to his grave.

In a mercifully short time, the consecrated soil began to do its work. His arms fell away from her, relinquishing their strangle hold on her neck, and the frantic bucking of his legs ceased as the soil leached the life away from him. As he succumbed to the inevitable, Cassie shifted the majority of her weight so that she wouldn't cause him any unnecessary pain.

It wasn't his fault someone had brought him back to use for their own purposes.

As he gave up his struggles, an oddly peaceful look came over what remained of his face. She held him down until he was completely drained, making sure there was nothing left in him to rise again.

Satisfied he was incapable of coming back to life, she vaulted easily out of the grave.

"Shit," she said, brushing the soil off her skin-molding black leather pants, "Why do all my dates have to turn out this way?"

She went over to check on Charlie. Still unconscious. Another trend that was becoming increasingly prevalent in her life. This would be the third time she'd have to haul an unconscious guy home - and that was just on this case. She braced herself to throw his weight over her shoulder.

At least he looked to be lighter than Striker.

A sudden rumbling caught her attention, followed by several more, all coming from different locations. Around her, the graves were boiling, dozens upon dozens of them churning as zombies struggled to rise.

This could be a problem.

She watched as heads and torsos broke free from the soil constraining them. There were at least fifty zombies heading her way, and at her best she had only taken on an even three dozen. Not to mention, she needed to find a way to keep Charlie safe while she was fighting.

Oh well, guess I'm going to have to go for a new record.

She rummaged in her bag, forsaking her blow torch for her favorite machete. "Who's first?"

She managed to take the first few out easily, lopping off bloodless arms and legs with little effort. The next dozen proved a little more difficult, as whoever was controlling them was intelligent enough to split them up, sending half after her and half after the unconscious Englishman. Cassie was forced to waste precious fighting time vaulting to his side and dragging him to safety. With a murmured apology, she tossed him into one of the open graves before resuming her attack. Most zombies were scared of graves, even if they weren't their own, so he should be safe down there.

"I'm getting old," she thought as she took the heads off two undead with a careless backhand swing. "I'm a little out of breath."

Let's see, how many are left? Two, three… no, make that four. Four dozen and more appearing every second. It's not looking good for the home team.

A flash of silver caught the corner of Cassie's eye. She maneuvered around to get a better look, sending the zombies currently trying to swarm over her flying in all directions.

I hope none of them landed on Charlie.

The flash was drawing closer, getting larger and brighter. As Cassie could make out more details, she could only stare in disbelief.

David was headed her way, and judging from

the sword in his hand and the scowl on her face, he wasn't there for a social visit.

Chapter Fifteen

"Just what does he think he think he's doing? He's going to get himself killed." Cassie watched as he moved through the zombie horde, his sword flashing in glittering arcs as he wove his way towards her. Surprisingly, he handled himself well. Even though he never took his eyes off her, he was easily dispatching the zombies that were breaking off to intercept him, knocking them aside with negligent ease.

One undead creature, either more intelligent or more desperate than its companions, jumped him from behind, clinging to his neck in an attempt to stop him. Without slowing or turning his head, David sent his sword flickering over his shoulder and sliced the zombie into two halves that fell harmlessly off to either side.

"Nice move." Cassie would have applauded, but her hands were a little full. David's appearance had spurred the zombies surrounding her to new extremes. Not wanting to be outdone, she split a few of them into pieces herself. "You're a little slow on the recoil, but you've got good wrist action and excellent extension," she called out to him.

His face was grim, anger and fear transforming

his handsome features.

He drew closer, dispatching a few more zombies on the way. "Why didn't you call me when the zombies showed up? You could have gotten killed."

"Sorry. I must have left my phone back at the car. I should have asked these guys if they had one I could borrow." A bubble of happiness rose in her chest as she wiped out the undead who was trying to rake its long, jagged nails across her face.

"From now on, I want you carrying it everywhere you go." David clubbed a zombie into submission with the pommel of his sword, "You can throw it in that ridiculously oversized bag of yours."

Okay, it was one thing to be mad at her for getting in a little over her head, but now he was questioning her fashion sense? "I need that bag for my investigations. And it goes perfectly with my boots, thank you very much."

He probably just couldn't tell because they were covered in zombie dust at the moment.

Besides, who is he to talk, anyway? He isn't exactly dressed for the runway in Milan, either.

"So, is the armor really necessary?" she asked, effortlessly dodging an overhand swing from an undead trying to bludgeon her with another undead's detached but still moving leg. "It's a little showy for daytime, you know."

Dented in several places and scorched in others, you couldn't exactly call the breastplate *shining* armor, but it wasn't exactly standard office wear.

"We had a couple suits lying around the house

and I thought one might come in handy when you found out I've been following you." His gaze flickered to a point over her shoulder. "Behind you."

"Thanks." She spun to take care of the zombie. "Normally I'd be pretty pissed, but in the circumstances, I think I'll let it go. Just don't let it happen again."

"Can't do that. I told you before, I won't interfere with your job, but I'm not going to stand by if you go into danger without backup. Get used to it. So, do you have a plan," he continued, "or are we winging it?"

"I was planning on taking out as many as I could with this." She brandished her machete, trying to pretend that several parts of her - *the main one being the spot beating irregularly in the middle of her chest -* hadn't warmed considerably at his statement. "Then I was crossing my fingers that my blowtorch had enough fuel for the rest. Since you're here, though, I suppose I would be willing to share. Four o'clock."

"Thanks." He speared the zombie on the point of his sword with a speed that sent a tremor of excitement through her. He turned so that his back was pressed up against hers, enabling them to see in a 360-degree circle. "What side do you want? East or west?"

"East. I like the way the sun highlights my hair from behind."

He nodded, and they circled around, positioning themselves to take on the oncoming horde.

She wasn't sure if it was David's presence or if

the puppet master was tiring, but the zombies seemed to be weakening. They fell before her machete with little to no effort on her part until bodies – and heads and limbs – were piled up before her. From what she could hear behind her, David wasn't having any harder of a time. Occasionally she would hear the rasp of his sword as it cut through the air, or the sound of his breath as he inhaled deeply and effortlessly.

Soon the onslaught trickled to a halt. After taking care of the last straggler, Cassie cleaned off her machete and looked around. There was an impressively large mound of now permanently dead undead at her feet. Still, she had to give credit where credit was due. The stack in front of David was almost as large. "You did pretty well with that sword."

"There's no reason to sound so surprised. I did tell you I beat Gideon a couple of times," he snapped.

So, not entirely happy with her, then. She couldn't blame him for that. "You said he let you win."

"I said he *might* have let me win." His jaw was clenched so tightly it looked painful. "But even if he did, I'm still a better fighter than Charles." His skin flushed, turning a mottled red. "What were you thinking when you choose to take him with you? What could he have done to protect you?"

"Okay, first of all, I don't need protection." She would have defeated the zombies without David. It just would have taken her longer.

A lot longer, she realized, tallying the bodies scattered on the ground.

"And secondly," she continued, "what else was I

supposed to do?" She took a deep breath. "I... I didn't want to break my promise to you, and Striker wasn't in any condition to go. Charlie wanted to come; he was the logical choice."

She didn't know David had moved until his voice came from beside her, low and intimate. "You could have asked me."

She shook her head insistently. "I couldn't." Unable to look at him, she pushed some of the spare body parts into an open grave with the tip of her boot. "Back at my room, before we got... sidetracked... you wanted to talk. I think we need to."

"Now? Here?"

"It's quiet, and I don't think we're likely to be disturbed."

"Fine." Out of the corner of her eye, she could see his shoulders heave in a heavy sigh. Picking up a detached arm, he placed it respectfully by the side of one of the fallen zombies. "But I can guarantee you're not going to like what I say."

"Why not?"

"You know how I said I wasn't jealous of Gideon?"

"Yeah?"

"I lied. I was."

Cassie was familiar with how betrayal felt. She could catalogue every second of the process, from the initial discovery and loss of breath to the moment the blood in her veins turned ice-cold as she realized it had happened again. But now, with David standing in front of her, strenuously avoiding her eyes, with his shoulders hunched up defensively and out-right admitting he'd lied to her, she realized she didn't feel any of it. She didn't know why he had lied, but she was sure he hadn't done it to hurt her.

She trusted him enough to let him explain. "About what?"

"It's not like I hated him," he said, picking up body parts and placing them at the foot of one of the open graves. Kneeling down in front of the stack, he began to sort through it, carefully placing matching pieces in their own separate groupings. He treated each limb with an unconscious dignity, handling them as gently as if their owners could still feel pain. "I could never do that."

"But you were jealous?" she asked.

He sat back on his heels. "Not at first... not when we were kids." His arms dropped to his sides and he gazed aimlessly out towards the horizon. "Not until I realized I could never have what he had."

"Which was?"

"He was always a better inventor than me. A better businessman, too. Sometimes it seemed like there was nothing he couldn't do." His hands came together on his lap, the fingers of his left hand twisting the ring on his right so hard she thought he was going to bruise himself. "But I told you the truth when I said I didn't resent him for any of that. I was proud of him."

"So what changed?"

"The Cataclysm."

Cassie shook her head, confused. "You were

only three when it happened. I thought you said you weren't jealous of him when you were young."

"I wasn't. But when I got older, when I realized why he had changed during the cataclysm and I hadn't... that's when it started."

"I get it," she said. "You felt like he was the special one. He got all the cool powers and you got nothing." It was a common complaint amongst those that were unaffected by the cataclysm, those that had been born before it but hadn't been old enough to experience their own transformations.

"Gideon was always so sure of himself, of who he was. I didn't want to take that away from him. I just wanted my own place, my own purpose." He turned his head, seeking her out. "A couple years ago, I started looking for it." One of his shoulders rose in a half-shrug. "I thought that if I found something I was good at, something I could believe in, maybe I could undergo a change of my own. No matter what I tried, though, nothing worked." A faint sheen of tears filled his eyes and he made no attempt to hide them. "I guess I figured I wasn't worthy."

The breath caught in her throat at the idea that the man in front of her had ever thought he wasn't good enough for anything.

"David, you had to have known how rare spontaneous transformations are." During the first few years after the Cataclysm, they had happened somewhat frequently, but after that wave had passed, they'd become far less common. Typically, they only occurred at puberty or other times of intense physical and psychological stress. "It's not a reflection on you."

His hands stilled. "I think I didn't tell you about Gideon taking my place on the trip to Spain because I didn't want to remember it. I didn't kill him," he said, "but he died because of me. Because I chose to run off on a wild goose chase instead of going on a business trip, my brother is gone." He looked at the ring on his finger. "I told that to Gideon when he came back. I told him how sorry I was... that I would never forgive myself. Do you know what he said?"

"What?" Cassie whispered, afraid to ask too loudly in case it shattered the fragile buds of hope sprouting in her heart.

A faint smile appeared on his face, barely lifting one corner of his mouth. "He said I hadn't done anything wrong. That he was proud of me for going after my dream, and he knew someday I'd find it." He brushed his hands off on his pants and rose to his feet. "And you know what? I did. After all these years of wondering," he said, standing in front of her with his shoulders set strong and proud, "I finally found my purpose."

"You did?" She was still having a hard time breathing, but it was for an entirely different reason. The tears in his eyes had faded, replaced by a fervent light that left her shaky. "What is it?"

His jaw firmed, casting his sculpted face into stark lines. "It's you, Cassie. You are my purpose."

David ran his hand roughly through his hair, pushing it out of his face. "The moment I saw you, I knew I was going to devote the rest of my life to you.

I know it sounds crazy, but it's true. I tried to take it slow at first, knowing I couldn't expect you to feel the same way - not so suddenly - but that night in the forest, I couldn't fight it any longer."

"If you want me to apologize, I will," he interrupted himself, "but I can't be sorry it happened. I thought it might be the only chance I'd ever have to be that close to you." His eyes burned with the same fire and intensity they had held that night, invoking a similar response from Cassie.

He stepped towards her and cupped her cheek with his palm. "I'll understand if you can't trust me after the things I've kept from you, but I need you to understand this." He drew himself up to his full height. "Whether you forgive me or not... whether I never get to touch or even see you again... meeting you has made my life worthwhile."

"David." Cassie found herself arching into his touch with a longing unlike anything she had ever experienced, "That is complete and utter bullshit."

"What?"

Her heart was pounding, drumming so loudly she could feel its heavy beat throbbing in her ears. "I chase dead things for a living, I've never had a relationship that lasted longer than six months, and I'm more comfortable in a firefight than cuddling. In what world could I possibly make anyone's life worthwhile?"

"In mine." His eyes shone with complete conviction. "In my world, you're perfect."

"That's insane." She rested her hands on his

upper arms, partly to steady herself and partly to try and shake some sense into him if she had to. "You're insane."

"Maybe," he agreed, placing his own hands just above the swell of her hips on either side and tugging her close enough that she could feel the cool metal of his armor brushing up against her skin. "I don't care."

God, the butterflies were back. And they'd brought friends. She could feel them swarming through her, leaving little pockets of happiness in their wake and making her feel like she was floating.

"David..." was all she managed say before he tilted his head and molded his lips to hers in a searing kiss.

Her hands tightened on his arms, enjoying the feel of his muscles under her fingers almost as much as she was enjoying the seductive caress of his mouth. She sank into the feeling, allowing the butterflies to fly free for one precious moment before drawing softly back from his embrace. "There's something you need to know." She nervously ran her palms down the legs of her leather pants. "When I said we needed to talk, I meant we both needed to come clean with each other. There's something I've been keeping from you. Something you have a right to know."

His eyebrows drew down in concern. "What's wrong? Did you get hurt in the fight? Do you need to see a doctor?"

"No, it's nothing like that." *God, she didn't want to do this.* "Do you remember how I said I've never been in a relationship for more than a few months?"

He nodded.

"Well, there's a reason for that. It's the same reason I've been drawing back from you..." She stammered, searching for the right words to tell him she was under a curse that would eventually turn him against her. "It's the same reason we can't get any closer until I fix a couple of things. Well just one thing, really, but it's a big one."

"Cassie, you're rambling." He was looking even more worried than he had before. "Whatever it is, it can't be that bad."

"You'd be surprised."

'Hello..." Charles voice floated up out of one of the graves. "Is anybody up there? I seem to have gotten into a bit of trouble."

Oh, thank God. Saved by the imbecile.

Cassie eagerly grasped the lifeline Charlie had unwittingly given her. "Uh, we should probably go help him."

"Allow me." David walked to the grave the voice had come from and jumped in. Seconds later, Charlie's head peeked over the edge, followed closely behind by the rest of him.

Cassie couldn't resist taunting him. "Glad to see you're okay, Charlie boy. Still want to live the life of a zombie hunter?"

Charles turned a whiter shade of gray. "I believe I've changed my mind. About many things."

"Aw, sad to hear it." She watched as David vaulted out of the open pit and started to walk towards them.

"Everything okay?" he asked, making sure the Englishman hadn't sustained any injuries.

"Yep, but Charlie here seems to be anxious to get home. We should get going."

David agreed, and the three began to make their way out of the cemetery.

"David, could we finish our conversation later? Maybe after we've all got some rest?"

"Sounds good to me." He fell into place walking by her side. "And Cassie?"

"Yes?"

"I know you said you don't want for us to get any closer until we solve whatever it is that's bothering you..."

""I *do*, but we *can't*."

"... But do you think it would be okay if I held your hand?" he asked with a hopeful grin.

The butterflies took flight again.

"I think maybe we can."

Chapter Sixteen

You would think that with the advent of the Cataclysm, people's beliefs would have become stronger. Oddly enough, it wasn't true. Even though they had witnessed fantastical transformations with their own eyes, some still refused to accept there was anything out of the ordinary about it. They attributed everything to random genetic flukes or dumb luck, and continued on their way, oblivious to the wondrous possibilities opening up around them. Very few individuals managed to grasp the idea that in this new world, anything you believed was theoretically possible.

And unfortunately, some of those who did understand it realized they could use it to their advantage...

***

After delivering Charlie to the house and making sure he was safely ensconced with the appropriate medical supervision, Cassie returned to her room to clean up. Forgoing the bathtub for expediency's sake, she hopped into the shower and let the multitude of showerheads do their work. As the water sluiced over her, washing away the remnants of graveyard dirt and undead debris, her thoughts flickered back and forth, skipping from David to the case and back again without any rhyme or reason. She knew she should be focusing solely on her work, but every time she tried to steer her focus in that direction, he would sneak back in.

One second she'd be planning ways to locate the puppet master who'd raised the zombies at the cemetery, and the next she'd be smiling at the memory of David fighting at her back, the two of them moving in perfect sync.

It didn't get any better when she finished the shower and dried off. She couldn't help thinking about the way he had looked at her – the way he'd stared at her with an expression she'd never seen before, his eyes darkening to the color of bittersweet chocolate - when he had said *she* was his purpose. It wasn't true, of course, but she couldn't stop the warm flush that spread throughout her, lightening her soul and setting fire to her heart.

She had never met anyone like him before. He was such an intriguing combination... a caring, gentle manner mixed with moments of unflinching courage and sheer animal magnetism. She'd tried to fight it, but she couldn't get him out of her system and deep down, she didn't want to. She wanted to get to know him and for him to get to know her.

But there was something she needed to do first. She'd put it off long enough.

She took her time choosing her outfit. It had to

be perfect, conveying the appropriate combination of, "I'm completely self-assured but not self-absorbed," and, "I ruin men's lives but I want you to take a chance on me, anyway." In the end, she chose a butter-soft pair of black denim, a burgundy silk blouse open to the second button, and a matching pair of high-heeled ankle boots.

He was waiting for her in the main parlor, sitting in a low backed Valencia leather chair. His legs were crossed with one foot resting on the knee of his other leg and his head was turned away from the door as he stared out the window. Sunlight streamed in through the window, giving him an angelic halo that seemed entirely appropriate.

Cassie drank in the sight. "Thanks for coming," she said.

"Cassie." His face lit up and he sprang to his feet. "There's nowhere I'd rather be."

She moved further into the room, her stomach clenching as she tried to figure out how to say what she needed to say.

Hello, nice to see you, by the way, did I mention I'm under a curse that's going to turn you against me?

She couldn't just blurt it out. Every time she tried to, her throat constricted and she felt like she was going to pass out from a lack of oxygen.

David must have sensed her discomfort, because he rushed to her side and took her arm, guiding her to a nearby settee. "Are you alright?" He knelt down in front of her, looking nervous as he continued. "You look pale. Are you sure you didn't get hurt in the fight?"

"No, I'm okay." He looked unconvinced, so she gave him her most reassuring smile. "Really, I am. I promise. I just got a little lightheaded. Breakfast seems like a long time ago."

"Let me get something for you."

"No." She put her hand on his arm, stopping him from rising. "It can wait. This can't."

His expression grew more concerned. "Cassie honey, I really think we should call the doctor." He took her wrist in his hand, his thumb resting on its soft underside to check her pulse. "I know you said nothing was wrong, but some injuries take a while to become noticeable."

"You're right." This injury was eight years old, and it had never been so painful. "Something is wrong." She turned her head away, staring at the tiny gold flowers embossed on the wallpaper so she wouldn't have to see the look on his face when he realized why he should run far away from her. "But it isn't anything a doctor can cure."

"Cassie, you're scaring me." Out of the corner of her vision, she could see him moving to take the seat next to her, still holding on to her wrist. His other hand reached out, moving slowly until his fingers threaded through her hair. "Will you look at me? Please?"

She shook her head. "I can't."

"Please."

Unable to resist, she turned his direction, their bodies angling together so their knees brushed against each other.

He let his hand slide down until it came to rest on her cheek. "Whatever it is, we'll find a way to stop it. I'm not going to let anyone or anything hurt you."

"You will." She closed her eyes so her tears wouldn't leak out. "You won't be able to help it because I'm under a curse."

There, she had done it.

"A curse? What kind?" She could hear the strain in his voice. "Is it fatal?

"No. It won't kill you."

"I didn't mean that. I meant you." His hand tightened around her wrist. "Will it kill you?"

"No. It doesn't do anything to me."

His grip on her wrist loosened. "Then what does it do?"

She took a deep breath before answering. "It changes people. People I... people I'm involved with," she whispered. "It would change *you*."

"So what, I'd turn into a werewolf or something?"

That's odd. He doesn't sound upset.

She opened her eyes.

He was still holding her wrist loosely in his hand. His thumb started to caress it, brushing back and forth. "Cause I've got to admit, being a were' sounds like it could be fun," he said, "especially if I get to chase you."

"That's not what it does!" she snapped.

'Then what?"

Why wasn't he taking this seriously? Didn't he

realize what she could do to him?

Of course he didn't. She hadn't told him the worst of it. "You don't get it." As his touch skimmed over her skin, it was becoming harder and harder for her to keep her mind on track, but she had to tell him. "I know you think I have something to do with your purpose..."

"You are my purpose." His nail grazed her pulse point, causing it to skip a beat.

"But it's not true," she stammered, barely holding on to her focus. "It can't be. My curse won't let it be."

"You keep saying that," he said, stroking the palm of her hand with his thumb and tracing her life and love lines. "But you haven't said why." He lifted her hand and brushed a kiss over the spot his thumb had been gliding over.

Oh God, what had she been saying again?

She wrenched her hand away so she could think straight. "Because no matter what you think of me now, it won't last. You're going to end up hating me. And when – not if, but when – you do, you'll end up betraying me," she said, rushing through the words to spare herself from imagining how it would feel when it inevitably happened. "And judging from past experience, you'll be happy to do it."

He drew back with an alarmed look on his face. "You're right. This is serious."

"I know. That's what I've been trying to tell you."

"You really think I would hurt you?"

"No. Not you." She was sure of that. He was incapable of cruelty. "But my curse would use you to do it."

"I don't believe it."

"I know it's a lot to accept. I didn't want to, either, but after the third or fourth time, I went to a shaman and he confirmed it. Since then, a friend and I have been looking into ways to break it, and I think we're close to figuring it out, but," she babbled, trying not to appear too hopeful, "I'll understand if you're not willing to take the chance."

His eyebrows drew down over worried eyes and he shook his head. "I'm not."

"Oh." His answer pierced her heart, transforming it into a lead ball that sunk to her stomach with a heavy thud. "Sure... of course. I guess I'll get going then."

He grabbed her hand before she could stand. "Cassie, sweetheart, I didn't mean I'm not willing to risk it... I meant there's no risk to take." The worry he had shown earlier was gone. Instead, there was something that looked suspiciously like laughter lurking in his eyes and at the corners of his mouth. "There is no possible way I'm ever going to betray you. You're worrying over nothing."

"I am not," she said, starting to get angry. He wasn't taking this seriously, and it was going to get them both hurt.

Laughter spilled out of him, lighting his face and making him appear even more handsome than usual.

The jackass.

He stared at her, the laughter in his eyes suddenly dying down to a warm, sweet light. "Cassie, honey, magic can't bring anything out of a person that isn't already there. There is nothing in this world or any other that could ever make me hate you." He closed the remaining space between them, resting his forehead against hers. "And I would die before ever betraying you."

Cassie's mouth went dry, and she swallowed nervously in a futile attempt to restore some semblance of normality. "Don't. Don't say that."

"It's true. I know you think your curse might change me, but I promise nothing is going to happen."

"Tell that to the legions of guys I've driven away. Not that there were *that* many," she hastily added. "I mean, I suppose it depends on how many you define as that many."

David smiled. "Cassie, I figured you had a past - most people do. But why would it bother me? It's made you who you are now. Although I've got to assume that if they were weak enough to let a measly curse get in the way of being with you," he continued, "then they weren't worth your time in the first place."

Oh, that was sweet. In fact, it was so sweet, she was almost willing to overlook that he was reckless enough to put himself into danger because of her. "You say that now...:

"I will always say it."

"But I don't want to risk it. I can't risk it." Clutching her hands together, she found her fingers tracing the spot where his thumb had caressed her palm. She could feel the warmth he had left behind, could feel the ghost of his touch on her. "I can't risk you."

"Then where do we go from here? Do you want me to keep my distance?" he asked, closing his eyes as if he was dreading her answer. "Because I'll do it if it's what you really want, but it's not going to change the way I feel about you."

"I don't want that."

"Oh, thank God." His eyes opened and he breathed a sigh of relief. "I'm not sure I would have been able to, anyway."

"Me neither." The thought of not being near him was enough to make her world as dull and joyless as a satyr without a wine bottle. "If you really want to try this..."

"I do." His answer came quick and certain, without a moment's hesitation.

Cassie flushed, her cheeks warming. "Then we need to take things slow until I can figure out a way to break the curse." God, he was too good to be true. She'd never been with someone this open... this *straightforward* before. "I have a friend who's helping me, so hopefully we won't have to wait too long."

"I'm willing to wait as long as you want. You're worth it."

She almost argued with him. Not because she didn't think she was a good person overall, but because no one could be worthy of the trust and patience he was offering her. Luckily, she wasn't stupid. She might not deserve him, but she was going to grab onto him with both hands and never let go. "Thank you." *And speaking of not letting go...* "Going slow doesn't mean we can't do anything at all, you know."

He pulled back from her with a hopeful smile. "It doesn't?"

"Nope. It doesn't." Threading her fingers through his hair and bringing him back where he belonged, she gave in to her desire and claimed what she had been aching for.

David responded eagerly, pouring himself into the kiss like his life depended on it. One moment they were two separate entities, and the next, their mouths were joined together, striving to know each other as deeply as they could. Teeth nipped and tugged, and hands came up to hold and caress.

Wrapped around him as if he was the only thing grounding her to the world, Cassie thought her heart was going to explode. It had never felt like this before. It had never been this intense... this right. It had never felt like friendship and lust and trust all wrapped up together.

The thought should have scared her, but it didn't. Putting her palm against his chest, she could feel his heart beating as strongly as hers, and she knew that whatever happened, he would be right there with her. She tightened her grasp.

She couldn't let him go. Not without a fight.

She kissed him again. And again. One kiss after another, melding into each other until the world around them disappeared in a haze.

"Ahem." A soft cough shattered their reverie and they pulled apart, breathing heavily. David's mother was standing in the doorway, looking both embarrassed and yet somehow pleased at the same time. "I'm so sorry, but there's a call for Cassie on the house line. I wouldn't have interrupted," she said, trying valiantly to hide the twinkle in her eyes, "but it seemed like it might be important."

Cassie flushed. "Oh, sure... thanks for letting me know." She raised her hand to straighten her hair, trying to pretend she hadn't just been caught making out with the other woman's son. "Uh, can I take it in here?"

"Of course." Diana pointed her in the direction of a lady's writing table. The phone, an old-fashioned rotary model updated to use modern technology, was resting on top. "And don't worry, I have some business that's going to take me out of the house, so you'll have complete privacy for the call... and anything else you'd need it for, of course." Chuckling quietly, she left the room.

Flushed with embarrassment, Cassie picked the receiver up. "Cassie here. What can I do for you?"

"Ms. Jones, it's Dr. Bedard. I thought you'd like to know Sasha is awake and feeling well enough for visitors."

Damn right she'd like to know. The deeper she got into this case, the more personal it was becoming. And not just because of David, although she couldn't deny he was a large part of it. Whoever was behind this was messing with people's lives. He or she had decided it was okay to play god, and as a result, people were getting hurt.

Gideon and his family. Sasha. Sasha's boyfriend.

Even the zombies who had been resurrected. They'd been ripped from their graves and set to work doing their puppet master's bidding, with no thought or concern as to their wishes or welfare. And it would only get worse if it wasn't stopped. Right now, as terrible as the guilty person's crimes were, they were limited to a local scale. If they got their hands on Gideon's invention, there would be no ends to the damage they could do. They could literally rule the world.

Hell, no. There was no way she was going to let that happen. Not before, when she was resigned to a life of somewhat-contentedly-ever-after, and certainly not now, when she had the possibility of so much more.

"We'll be right over," she said, not wanting to waste a minute. "Thanks for the call." Placing the old-fashioned receiver back in its cradle, she hung up, her mind already busy formulating the questions she wanted to ask Sasha.

"Who was that?" David's voice pulled her out of her reverie. He was perched on the edge of the desk, making sure he didn't crowd her, but even though there wasn't any physical contact, she could feel the current of energy present between them.

"It was the hospital. Sasha is ready to talk."

A broad smile broke over his face. "That's great.

Are you going to go see her?"

Cassie shrugged. "I thought we could both go. They say two heads are better than one, right? And you've gotten to know her since she'd been in the hospital. That might come in useful."

"Are you sure? I don't want to interfere."

"You won't."

"Then I'll get the car." He darted out of the room and went to make the necessary arrangements.

The wheels were turning in Cassie's head. There was no doubt in her mind John had been assisting Gideon in his project. He'd provided the polymers, and who knows what else. If Sasha could tell them what those polymers were...

David poked his head in through the door. He held out his hand like a gallant courtier assisting his liege. "Your chariot awaits, milady."

"Fine." She placed her hand in his. "But I'm driving."

"Anything you say."

The more he said it, the more she was beginning to like the sound of that.

***

The hospital didn't look any different to the way it had the last time they were there. It had the same workers rushing around trying to look busy, and the same horny cyclops stationed at the nurse's desk. The only real difference was that the cyclops was now an unhappy witness to David holding Cassie's hand as they made their way through the corridors.

Eat your heart out, sweetie. He's with me.

Dr. Bedard was waiting for them, filling them in on her patient's condition as she escorted them to Sasha's room.

"We don't believe she suffered any permanent danger from the attacks," she said, getting straight to the point. "Her physical injuries are responding well to treatment, and she's starting to regain some of her lost memories." She paused to scratch behind her ear with a hand even more densely coated with hair than it had been on their previous visit. "Please excuse me," she said with a grimace, "I'm having a bad fur day today."

"Here, this might help." Cassie pulled a pretty pastel colored bottle from her bag. She had made sure to throw it in before leaving the castle. "My friend Ash swears by this stuff. She says it keeps the itch away, plus it gives her a coat a nice glow."

"Thanks," the doctor said, taking the gift with pleasure. "I'll give it a shot. Now, as I was saying," she continued as they walked, "Sasha has started to recollect what happened to her. As I mentioned on the phone, she's already told us a few things, but I believe you should hear the rest directly from her."

"Do you think she's ready to talk about it?" David asked. "We don't want to push her if it will interfere with her recovery."

"In my professional opinion, the sooner she deals with what happened, the sooner she will be able to move on from it." She stopped outside room number 815. "We're here."

She tapped on the door.

"Come in," a pleasant voice called from inside, and David opened the door, holding it for the two women.

As she passed by him, Cassie couldn't help but brush up against his chest with her own. Well, she could have helped it, but she didn't want to. It was such a good chest, and judging from the light that sparkled in his eyes, the feeling was mutual.

"Sasha, you remember David, I'm sure," Dr. Bedard said. "This is Cassie Jones, the woman I told you about."

Sasha smiled, the dimples on either side of her mouth making her appear even more out of place in the sterile confines of the hospital room. With her small frame and open face, she looked as if she should be out frolicking in a grassy meadow, not sitting in a hospital bed and wrapped in bandages.

"Hello David, Miss Jones." Her voice was light and airy, too, and Cassie surreptitiously looked to see if her ears were pointed. If Sasha didn't have elf blood in her, Cassie would wear polyester jumpsuits for a year.

"Thank you for agreeing to see us." She took a seat next to the injured woman's bed, and David moved to stand behind her, resting his hand on Cassie's shoulder. "I know you've been through a lot."

"I don't understand any of this," Sasha said, the smile disappearing from her face and leaving confusion and pain behind. "No one can tell me why this is happening."

"We were hoping you could tell us."

"I can't. It doesn't make any sense." She struggled to sit up, her face paling as she did so. "I've heard of zombies attacking in the wild before, but John and I were on public park land. And why would it follow me here to the hospital?"

Cassie leaned forward. "We aren't sure it did. It may have been two separate zombies."

"No." Sasha shook her head. "It wasn't. I recognized it." She was struggling to maintain her composure, but Cassie could see the effort it was costing her. "It was the same one," she said, waving off the doctor's attempts to make her lie back down again.

"Why didn't you mention this to the police?"

"I didn't remember. It wasn't until it attacked me here that I started to have flashbacks." She shifted uneasily, her gaze darting away as if she were afraid to have another one. "Seeing it again must have triggered them."

"Can you describe it?" David blurted out, his hand tightening on Cassie's shoulder. "What did it look like?

Sasha shivered. "Like a monster." She wrapped her arms around herself. "It didn't have any hair, and I could see its skull where the skin had pulled away from its face, but the worst was its eyes. The way they looked at me like I didn't matter... like nothing mattered." She shook her head and drew tighter into herself. "There was nothing human to it at all."

Definitely not Gideon, then. It had to be an older zombie, one far less sentient and far more decomposed.

Cassie could feel the tension draining out of David as he relaxed his grip. She wanted to tell him how happy she was that Sasha's words had confirmed his brother's innocence, but it would have to wait until later when they were alone. Right now, she owed a duty to the woman in front of her.

It was a sentiment David apparently shared. He moved from behind Cassie and took a place at her side. "It's okay," he said, placing his hand on top of Sasha's trembling one. "It's gone now. You're safe."

She looked up at him with red rimmed eyes. "But what if it comes back? There's nothing I can do to stop it."

"That's not true. You already have. Twice," Cassie pointed out. "You managed to survive both attacks."

"Barely." Her hands fisted in the blanket covering her lap. "And John didn't." She turned to Cassie. "Dr. Bedard told me that you're trying to find him… the one responsible for John's death."

"I am."

"I want him to pay for everything he's done. I want him to suffer. Will you do that?" she asked, looking as if, for all of her frail appearance, she would rise up and seek her own vengeance if the answer was no.

Fortunately, she wouldn't have to. There was no way Cassie was going to deny her request. "I'll find whoever was responsible for your boyfriend's death, and I promise I'll make him or her pay for the full extent of his crime. But I'm afraid it might not be as simple as finding one zombie. We have reason to believe it was being controlled by someone else."

"I know it was," Sasha snapped. "That's who I'm talking about. Not the zombie."

"You know? How?"

"I saw him. At the campsite."

Cassie felt a jolt of excitement course through her. "You saw him? What can you tell us?"

"Not much, unfortunately. It's still pretty hazy, but every now and then something will jog my memory. I remember seeing the zombie by the campfire... it was standing over John, and it seemed so mad. It was tearing at his clothes, and I remember thinking I had to stop it before it hurt him..." Tears began to run down her face. "I didn't realize he was already dead."

Cassie pulled a tissue from her bag and pressed it into the other woman's hand. "What happened next?"

"I think I must have moved or said something, because it left John and came after me. I don't know what happened then... it hurt so much and I just remember trying to get away... and then I heard someone yelling." She paused, shredding the tissue in her hands to tiny pieces. "I thought it was over, that someone had come to save us." She stared at the tissue fragments piled in front of her, fingers searching aimlessly for a piece large enough to tear.

"But he never came closer. He just kept arguing with the zombie, telling it to get back to work. I think the zombie might have thrown something at him, but I'm not sure. I'm sorry. I'd like to tell you more, but it hurt so much…"

"You noticed more than most people would have in the situation," David said gently. "Do you think you would be able to describe what the person looked like?"

"No. I just heard his voice, and even that was muffled. I'm sorry. I should have been paying better attention. I should have done something…"

"Don't," Cassie said. "You did all you could. You can't blame yourself."

"But if I had fought harder… or if I'd stayed in camp and hadn't gone on a walk…"

"Then both of you might be dead. There was nothing you could have done for John then, but there's something you can do now. I need you to tell me everything about what he said to you about this trip. We know he'd been here before, and that he'd previously done business here, but what about this time? Did he meet with anyone?"

"No."

Cassie handed her another tissue. "Are you positive?"

"Yes." She wiped her face, her tears drying as Cassie refocused her away from her boyfriend's death and onto the hunt for his killer. "We had just gotten to the campsite that day. John never went anywhere by himself, and no one came to see us before the attack."

"Could he have planned to meet someone later?"

"I don't think so. He wasn't here for business; we were celebrating."

"Celebrating what?"

"John had been playing around with something for years. I'm not sure what it was – he never took it too seriously, he'd just laugh and tell me it was a pipe dream whenever I asked him – but he'd made a breakthrough recently. The money he got from it was enough to put a down payment on a house and pay for this trip."

Cassie turned to look at David.

"And you don't know what the breakthrough was?" he asked.

"I'm sorry, but I don't. He'd sent the specifications to the client months ago, and he hadn't mentioned it since. Even if he did try to tell me, though, I probably wouldn't have paid any attention. I never could get into amphiphilic polymers like he did – I was always more into theoretical polyhedrals."

Dr. Bedard spoke up from the corner of the room. "Do you have many more questions? I don't want Sasha over-exerting herself."

"I don't have too many more," Cassie assured her, "but it's important we get answers as quickly as possible."

"It's alright. I want to do whatever I can to help."

"You're doing great. Just a few last things before we go." She didn't want to push the young girl past her breaking point. "Do you have any idea what the compound was for?"

Sasha's expression clouded over. "I'm afraid not, but I imagine you could have it examined to find out its chemical makeup."

"We would if had some of it," Cassie said.

"But I do. Have some, I mean." At the looks of shock on everyone's faces, her own grew surprised. "John had a vial of it designed into a locket for me. I'm not sure where it's at right now, but I know I had it on when they brought me to the hospital."

Chapter Seventeen

It had only taken fifteen minutes to locate the envelope holding the jewelry Sasha had been wearing when she'd been admitted to the hospital. It had taken even less time to confirm the locket and its contents were nestled safely inside.

One short drive later, and Cassie and David were back at the MacDuff's family estate, searching for the last piece of the puzzle.

"Do you think it really could work?" David asked as he pulled out a drawer and knocked on its bottom to make sure there weren't any hidden compartments.

"I think there's a pretty good chance," Cassie answered. She had filled David in on Gideon's pet project on the way back to the house, and had shared her theory that it was the reason behind Gideon's death and resurrection. Now the two were ransacking Gideon's office to see if they could find proof. "You said your brother was a genius when it came to figuring out how to invent things." She upended the contents of the file cabinet in front of her onto the floor. "Now that we have the polymer, all we have to do is figure out how Gideon put the whole thing together. He has to have notes somewhere. The question is - where did he hide them?"

One thing is for sure, he didn't stash them here. They had searched thoroughly and hadn't found anything. The cabinet had been the last place left to check. The notes hadn't been in his bedroom, his former lab, or the labs of the other scientists, either.

"You're sure there was nowhere else Gideon used to go?"

"No." David was adamant. "He spent most of his time in his lab, here in his office, or working out at the cottage." He fit the drawer back in its place, making sure everything was put back neatly.

Cassie would have been content to leave the contents of the file cabinet lying on the floor, but she crouched down to help him. Even cleaning was more interesting when she was doing it with David.

"What about women?" she asked, savoring the thrill of being so close to him. "Were there any women Gideon spent a lot of time with? Ones who might hide something for him?"

"Not that I can think of. He played the field a lot when he was younger, but for the past five years, he said he didn't have time for it." His hand brushed hers as the reached for the same piece of paper. He smiled broadly, staring down at where their hands met. "It's funny... I always thought he was the lucky one, but I was wrong." He reached out to link his fingers with hers. "He never had someone like you in his life."

Shit. Every time she thought she was getting a handle on this whole relationship thing, David would go ahead and say something to make her melt even more.

"Hands off, handsome," she complained, trying to disguise the hopelessly sentimental warble in her voice. "Remember your promise. Until we solve the case and my curse, we take it slow and steady."

David squeezed her hand. "I'm trying to, but you make it difficult to think about anything other than drawing you into a dark, secluded corner where I could strip off..."

"Enough!" Cassie cutting him off before she could let her subconscious begin to imagine what he would be stripping... and how it would taste covered in chocolate sauce.

"We've got to be missing something," she said, reluctantly pulling her hand away. "We haven't found anything but cobwebs."

David stood up and filed the ream of papers away. "We haven't checked the cottage."

"I searched that place from head to toe when I thought you were hiding Gideon there, remember?"

"You were looking for a full-grown man. It wouldn't hurt to give it another look."

Makes sense. Gideon's notes probably wouldn't take up a lot of space; she might have missed them during her search. *Who knew David was handsome **and** smart?*

"You might be right," she told him. "It's worth a try, anyway. And maybe you could ask one of the legions of cooks your family employs to make us up some sort of snack to take with us?" They'd been searching all morning, and the huevos rancheros they'd shared for breakfast were only a distant memory.

"It would be my pleasure. I'll have them pack a picnic lunch. How does champagne, fruit, and cheese sound?"

"Like a little piece of heaven wrapped up in a plaid blanket."

"If you like that," David said with a wicked grin that made Cassie's heart dance a samba, "just wait till you see what's for dessert."

As soon as he was out of earshot, she dialed Ash's number. Her friend had barely picked up before Cassie launched into her request. "Tell me you've found something."

"Actually, I have." Ash's voice was curiously subdued. "I should have called sooner, but I didn't think you'd want to hear this. It's not good, Cass."

Cassie's heart stuttered. "Tell me."

"It wasn't easy, but Mom and I managed to track down the wizard who cursed you. I don't think we'd have been able to do it at all if she hadn't left such a big trail of casting similar curses."

"So she's a serial offender?"

"She was."

Cassie clutched the phone tightly. "Was?"

"She'd dead, Cass. She passed away two years ago."

Cassie flinched. "So... I don't suppose there's any chance the curse died with her, is there?"

"Not according to the other victims. All of them said the same thing - no cessation of the curse's effects. If anything, they've gotten worse."

Silence crackled over the connection.

"Cass…" Ashley hesitantly asked, "Are you going to be okay?"

"Sure. Of course I am." Silent tears ran down her face. "Really, it's not a big deal. It was a long shot, anyway. Thank your mom for all the hard work she did for me."

"Don't worry about it; you know she'd do anything for you. And we'll keep looking. We're bound to find something else. Some sort of loophole."

"Yeah, maybe." Cassie had to get off the phone before she lost it completely. "Someone's coming in, Ash, I'll talk to you later. Bye."

She hung up without giving her friend a chance to respond.

It was just like she'd feared. There was nothing she could do. She could almost hear the little voice crowing in her ear - the same one that woke her up in the middle of the night, whispering that she should just give up trying - telling her, "I told you so," over and over again.

Bullshit. If she was going to pay attention to any of the voices in her head, she'd damn well choose which one to listen to. *And I'm going with the one that's telling me not to let David go.* After all, if she wasn't willing to fight for her happy ending, she didn't deserve it in the first place.

And she was very, very good at fighting.

Blinking the tears from her eyes, she pulled a compact out from her bag and repaired the damage to her makeup. David would be coming back soon, and she didn't want him seeing her upset. Especially not now that they were so close to solving Gideon's murder and finding his invention.

Reaching into her pocket, she felt for the locket Sasha had lent her. Dr. Bedard had kept some of the compound for analysis, but Cassie had the other half. Just enough to trigger a controlled transformation once they found Gideon's notes, ending Cassie's curse once and for all.

David poked his head in through the door. "The picnic basket is loaded up. Are you ready?"

Cassie smiled. "Just try and stop me."

***

Cassie and David searched the cottage thoroughly.

Nothing. Absolutely nothing. They hadn't found a single thing that looked promising. There was nothing in the kitchen or the weapon's room, all of the closets were empty, and there were no tables with hidden drawers or conspicuously placed steamer trunks. She dropped to her knees beside the bed in Gideon's room and lifted the coverlet to check the floor underneath. There were a few twigs and leaves that his shoes must have trailed in from outside, but nothing out of the ordinary.

"I don't understand," she said, dropping the dark blue blanket back into place. "He must have left his notes somewhere."

David extended his hand and helped her to her feet. "Maybe he has them with him."

"I don't think so." Or at least, she hoped not. "Although if we don't find it here, we'll have to consider the possibility." She knocked on the wall behind the bed, listening for the dull sound that indicated a hidden recess. When that failed, she turned her attention to the bed itself. It was built solidly, made of heavy oak and careful craftsmanship, although personally, Cassie would have forgone the decorative riveting that studded the headboard. It was a little fussy for her taste.

Huh. Gideon hadn't struck her as the fussy type... Could it be?

She prodded at the headboard, trying to pry it loose, but it didn't want to give. "I need a crowbar."

David stepped behind her, and she could feel the heat radiating from his body as he wrapped his arms around her. "I'm surprised you didn't bring one with you," he said, laughter bubbling under the surface of his velvet-warm voice. "You have everything else in that monstrosity you call a handbag."

"Are you seriously insulting my accessories again?" The way he was nuzzling at her neck made it hard to be too angry. "Just for that, I'm going to make you get the crowbar from it."

He laughed. "You did bring one?"

"Yeah, but it's a bitch to find. It has a tendency to sink to the bottom."

He stopped nuzzling and started grazing on her

neck instead. "I've got a suggestion."

Yes. Whatever it is… Yes.

"Uh-huh…"

"I'm finding it a little hard to concentrate on behaving myself."

"Yeah, I noticed." She shivered as his teeth lightly scraped over her clavicle. "So?"

"So if I'm going to keep my promise, I should probably go get a breath of fresh air." His tongue smoothed the area his teeth had roused. "Why don't you look for the crowbar while I set up our lunch?"

"Sounds good to me." God knows, if he kept doing that, there was no way she was going to be able to keep her hands off of him until she found Gideon's invention and removed her curse. "But don't think my bag or I are going to forget what you said about it."

He was laughing as he left the room. Cassie had to admit she could grow used to the sound.

Sure enough, the crowbar had settled in the detritus at the bottom of the bag, nestled among empty candy wrappers, throwing stars, loose change, hermetically sealed microscope slides, and a half-empty perfume bottle.

"Alright, let's see what this thing can do."

She set to work on the first bolt. It didn't come easily – the bolt was wedged so tightly that the crowbar, sturdy as it was, seemed more likely to break than the fastening. When the bolt finally did release its grip, it flew across the room, hitting the far wall with a metallic 'ping.' Developing a rhythm, the others soon followed. By the time she had removed half of them, a faint line had appeared in the wood, running in a distinctly suspicious pattern. She picked up her pace, and the crack widened, until, at last, the rivets had all been removed and a small compartment, no larger than the size of both her hands put side by side, had been revealed.

Nestled inside was a tiny pouch.

"David, get in here," she yelled. "I think I've found something."

Without waiting for him, she started to inch the pouch out. She took it slowly, not wanting to jostle its contents - without knowing what they were, she wasn't about to risk anything breaking or exploding on her. Carefully, she lifted the flap.

"Bingo," she cried with an air of triumph. *No notes, but possibly something better.*

Three tiny, stoppered vials, each containing a different colored liquid – one a pale silver, one a coppery red, and the third an electric yellow - sparkled before her. Even in the shadowed interior of the pouch, they glowed with an incandescent light. Cassie was willing to bet they were the same chemical composition as the droplets they had found in the barn.

She pulled the locket Sasha had given her out of her pocket. "Now, exactly how does the polymer figure in?"

"I'll be more than happy to show you." A low voice accompanied by the distinct sound of a gun being cocked interrupted her thoughts. "Just hand it over, nice and slow."

Cassie looked up to see the barrel of a Hi-Point 9MM aimed directly at her - held in a very steady and very familiar hand. The last time she had seen the owner of that hand, she had been hauling his unconscious body to safety.

That would teach her not to make the same mistake twice.

Chapter Eighteen

Deep down, every criminal believes they are a Mastermind.

***

"Striker, I'd say it was nice to see you, but under the circumstances..." She tried to keep her voice calm, but it was a struggle. "Where's David? What did you do to him?"

"Worried about your boyfriend?" Striker laughed, his handsome face twisted into a snarled grin. "Don't be. He's fine. As a matter of fact, he invited me in, didn't you, Davey?"

At Striker's words, David entered the room. "I'm sorry, Cassie. I didn't realize... I thought he could help us. I didn't notice the guns until it was too late." In addition to the Hi-Point in his right hand, Striker was holding a gleaming Colt Revolver in his left hand, its muzzle aimed straight at David.

Cassie's heart skipped a beat before thudding painfully back into motion. Deep down, she'd known David wasn't the one responsible for Gideon's death, but at the moment she almost wished he had been guilty. Then he wouldn't be in danger because of her mistake.

"It's okay," she told him, kicking herself for not realizing the truth earlier. "It's not your fault. I didn't suspect him either." She should have, but the thought had never crossed her mind. She'd been so worried about the possibility of David betraying her, that it had never occurred to her to suspect anyone else. "I'm the one who fucked this up."

Striker snorted. "Like either one of you could have figured it out. I've been miles ahead of you from the start. Now, you," he snapped, motioning to David, "on the floor or I shoot you both – starting with her."

David raised his hands above his head and sunk to his knees. "I'll do whatever you want. Just let her go."

"Why would I do that? She's the one who has what I want." With his guns still trained on them, he smiled arrogantly. "When I first heard Davey was going to hire an investigator, I'll admit I got a little worried, but it turns out bringing you here was the best thing he could have done for me. Now hand it over."

"I don't know what you're talking about," Cassie said.

"The hospital called the house looking for you. It seems their lab is having problems analyzing the sample you left with them. They were wondering if they could have a little more of the part you'd kept for yourself." He extended his hand towards her. "Set it on the ground and send it over nice and easy or I put a bullet in his skull."

Knowing she had no other choice, she followed his instructions, using the tip of her red stilettos to push the small locket towards him.

"Very good." He crouched down to pick it up.

Out of the corner of her field of vision, Cassie could see David shifting his weight as if he were preparing to leap at the other man.

"David, don't," she said, knowing it would draw Striker's attention to him, but knowing she had to do it anyway.

Sure enough, the barrel of the Colt came up, aimed directly at David's heart. "Go ahead. Give me an excuse to pull the trigger," Striker snarled.

David stilled instantly, confusion and disbelief in his eyes as he looked from Cassie to Striker and back again.

She shook her head. "It's not worth our lives," she explained. "He's got us where he wants us. There's no point fighting him."

If they had an advantage, that would be a different story, but she wasn't about to take a needless risk – especially when it came to David's life.

Striker laughed. "You've got more sense than I gave you credit for. Pity your boyfriend doesn't. Here," he said, lowering the Hi-point and tucking it in the waistband of his pants before grabbing the pair of police grade handcuffs hanging on his belt. "Put these on him. Arms behind his back – and loop them around the leg of the bed."

"Whatever you say." He tossed them to her

and she knelt down beside David, cuffing his wrists together and being careful not to pinch his skin. Trying to communicate everything she couldn't say out loud, she brushed her thumb over his palm.

He let out a long shiver as if he were in pain and closed his eyes for a second, but when he opened them again, they were clear and unguarded, staring at her with complete trust.

She found herself shivering, astounded he could have such faith in her even after she had screwed up this case so badly. Squeezing his hand briefly, she silently promised herself she would do whatever it took to live up to that faith.

"Enough already. Move away from him." Striker ordered. "I didn't bring another set of cuffs, so I'll have to trust you. But make one move I don't like and his parents will have more than one zombie in the family."

David made a strangled noise at Striker's comment, but Cassie placed her hand on his shoulder to stop him from speaking.

"How could you do this to them?" she asked, drawing Striker's attention. "They consider you part of their family."

"They should have been my family. And they could have been – if the Cataclysm hadn't messed everything up for me."

"I don't understand." She took a half-step towards him. "What has the Cataclysm got to do with it?"

"Do you know who my father was? Before

the Cataclysm, he was one of the premier leaders in thermodynamics. He was a genius, more brilliant than even Malcolm or Diana at their greatest." The hand holding the gun wavered slightly, the barrel's aim moving from David's chest to his head before dipping back down again. "But he never got the chance to build the legacy they did, because the Cataclysm changed him. It made him something he wasn't supposed to be."

"What did he become?" she asked, inching closer. *If she could take him out now, she wouldn't have to do something she knew she'd regret in the long run.*

"Ordinary." The corner of his mouth curled up in a vicious snarl as he stared at her. "Instead of spending time in the lab where he belonged, he started spending it at home. Instead of striving to make scientific breakthroughs, he wanted to 'make memories' – as if memories ever won anyone a Nobel prize. And worst of all, he suckered Mom into going along with it."

"It doesn't sound so bad to me." *She was almost there. A few more steps and she could make a move without risking David...*

"Maybe for someone like you it wouldn't, but it was supposed to be different for me. They were supposed to open doors for me... to give me something I could be proud of... but the only thing they left me with was a few boxes full of crappy photos. Well," he grinned coldly, "Maybe not the only thing. At least Mom had the courtesy to get me an "in" with Malcolm and Diana. An in which I took full advantage of, even if they never saw me as anything more than dumb muscle."

Before Cassie could close the rest of the distance to Striker and disarm him, David called out, "That's not true! They love you."

"Yeah, right." Striker turned to face him fully, halting Cassie's plan until she could draw his attention away again. "That's why the sons of the manor are running the business while I got offered a job as the head of the goon squad. But that'll change as soon as I recreate Gideon's formula. I figured out how to make most of it from his notes, but since you've been thoughtful enough to find the solvents pre-made, I might as well make use of them. Now toss the pouch over."

With no other choice, Cassie did what he asked, watching as he caught the bag easily. He shrugged off the backpack slung over his shoulder, then crouched down to pull out a couple of beakers and a small Bunsen burner, keeping the Colt trained on David the entire while. He began to assemble the equipment, mixing vials and setting them over the burner with easy movements.

He was distracted, but not enough.

"You had his notes all along, didn't you?" she asked, knowing he wouldn't be able to resist bragging. "That's why we couldn't find them."

"Of course. He gave them to me for safekeeping. Didn't want "the wrong eyes" seeing them. It never even occurred to him that I'd be able to read them, let alone figure out what to do with 'em."

"He trusted you," David said, pulling against his bonds with a tug strong enough to send a tremor through the bed's frame.

"He shouldn't have. Then again, he shouldn't have trusted you, either," he said, smiling as David struggled with his bonds, pulling at the heavy leg of the bed that kept him chained in place, "After all, he was going to figure out the exact formula sooner or later, and when he did, I'd have been waiting to take it from him. But then you had to go and screw things up by forcing him to take your place in Spain. Funny, huh? Gideon started his research because he wanted to give you the chance to choose your own destiny, and in the end, it was all your fault he got killed."

Cassie felt sick to her stomach. How could she not have seen it? "You were trying to kill David, weren't you?"

"Nice guess, but wrong again," Striker laughed. "I didn't want either one of them dead. I needed Gideon to keep working and Davie was his motivation. The car cash screwed up all my plans."

"Then who caused it?" she asked.

"How the hell should I know? For a while, I thought maybe the wuss over there," he said, gesturing to David, "might have grown some balls and done something interesting, but he's still as boring as ever."

While he was looking at David, Cassie took another step towards Striker. "But the attack at the campground... you were behind that? You summoned the zombie that attacked Sasha and killed her boyfriend?"

"It was supposed to keep him alive 'till he told me what the missing polymer was, but things got out of hand."

"And Sasha?"

"I couldn't take the chance she'd remember seeing me there. When I heard you were going to interrogate her, I sent the zombie to make up for its previous mistake. It wasn't hard to smuggle it in – after all, who do you think Malcolm and Diane asked to set up hospital security?"

"Impressive. But what about the other attacks? You couldn't have had anything to do with them – you got hurt."

"That's what I wanted you to think. The zombies that attacked us were a set-up. I went into the woods to give them their orders. When I came out, they were supposed to see you running and take after you." She could hear the jagged edges in his voice. For all he wanted to believe he was in control, she could tell he was getting frustrated.

Frustration she wanted to encourage. "But I didn't run."

"You can't do anything right," he snapped, his hand tightening around the gun's handle. "I tried to signal them to kill you anyway, but they were too brain-dead to understand." His aim was becoming erratic, the gun's nozzle slowly moving back and forth between David and Cassie. "The one at the barn was supposed to kill you, too. You were so busy looking for clues, you didn't even notice when I summoned it.

And if that stupid ghost wouldn't have gotten in the way, it would have worked."

She shrugged. "It might have. It almost did at the cemetery, but I guess the third time wasn't exactly a charm for you, was it?" she goaded, hoping to anger him enough to push him the final step into carelessness. "For all your so-called brilliance, none of your plans seem to be working out too well."

She waited for his reaction, praying that in his anger he would turn the gun fully on her, but her comment seemed to have had the opposite effect.

His body relaxed, the gun swinging firmly back to David. "I don't know about that," he said calmly. "If you had gotten killed, you wouldn't have found the polymer for me. Sounds to me like the universe is finally making sure I get what I deserve."

Shit. Playing to his insecurities wasn't going to work. He was too stupid to realize just how stupid he was. *She really hadn't wanted to resort to this. She just hoped David would forgive her.*

"I think you might be right." She let her gaze sweep over Striker, starting at his muscular shoulders and dipping down to the tight fit of his jeans before moving back up again. "I'm beginning to think I underestimated you."

"Of course you did. Everybody does."

"Will Gideon's formula really let you have anything you want?"

"It's my formula now, not his," he growled. "I'm the one finishing what he couldn't."

"But it will work?" she prodded.

"Yeah."

"Then the only thing I want to know is..." she asked, drawing a deep breath for courage, "What do I have to do for you to let me use it, too?"

"Cassie, no!" David cried, pulling at his bonds again in an effort to get to her.

"I'm sorry, David, but you of all people should understand why I'm doing this. Striker's got a point about the Cataclysm screwing things up. If it weren't for it messing around with people's lives, none of this would have happened. Striker would be where he deserves to be, Gideon would be alive, and maybe I would have my own happily-ever-after instead of just watching other people get theirs. I don't approve of what Striker's done, but when all is said and done, he didn't kill your brother. Maybe there's a way we can all walk out of this with what we want."

"You can't do this!" David's continued his struggle to reach her. "He may not be behind Gideon's murder, but what about John and Sasha and all the other people he's hurt?"

"I can't worry about that. I've got to focus on what's right for me." It wasn't how she'd wanted this to go, but she didn't have a choice. "What's right for both of us. Don't you see... this might be our only chance."

He flinched. "Not like this, Cassie." He was staring at her as if she was breaking his heart, his warm brown eyes darkened by pain. "We can find another way."

"I'm sorry, David. We can't." Her heart felt like

it was fissuring into a thousand pieces. It was funny - she'd never been on this end of betrayal before.

She hadn't expected it to hurt so much.

She turned to Striker. "Tell me what you want and it's yours."

"NO!!" David pulled against his restraints with all of his strength. The bed lurched, giving a heavy thump, but no matter how hard he fought, he couldn't free himself.

Striker laughed at his struggles. "Very touching, but I don't believe any of it," he said, looking towards Cassie. "I'm not stupid enough to trust your sudden change of heart."

Cassie shook her head. "It's not a change of heart. I'm just tired of fighting things I can't win against. This is my best chance at getting what *I* want."

Striker took his time, looking first at her, and then at David's increasingly frantic effort to break free before answering her. "Alright," he said, grinning lasciviously, "I like a challenge, and it might be fun to show Davie over there how far you're willing to take this. Come over here."

She stepped closer, placing her hand on his forearm and dropping her voice to a more intimate pitch. "Whatever you need."

He plucked her hand from his sleeve, dropping it brusquely. "Thanks, but not interested. I'm not willing to settle for anyone willing to settle for him," he said, waving his gun at David. "I'll never understand it. He wasn't changed by the Cataclysm, and he's not anything special, but he got everything I should have had. Well, I'm going to take it back, and you're going to help me."

"I won't do anything to hurt him." She was willing to do some unpleasant things, but that wasn't one of them. "He and I both walk out of here alive. That's the deal."

"Oh, he won't be hurt. He'll be perfectly fine." With a flourish, Striker poured the polymer into the mixture simmering over the burner. "He'll be happier than he's ever been." The liquid in the burner changed colors, turning a luminescent shade of green. "After all, he won't have to deal with living up to his family's reputation anymore."

"You're going to take his place." In a sick way, it made sense. With the power of the Cataclysm behind him, Striker could rewrite history. No one would notice he had assumed David's place in the family; no one would remember it had ever been any other way.

"Nah..." Striker laughed. "Why would I do that when I can be the sole heir to the MacDuff family dynasty? I'm going to erase him and his brother entirely. But don't worry, I'll make sure you like the changes I make. Hell, I'll even let you make some of them. Be a good girl and do what I say, and you can turn him into whatever you want."

"Cassie, you can't! Don't do this!" David screamed, pulling against his bonds so hard that the cuffs dug into his skin, tearing the skin underneath.

She ignored his outburst, pushing the pain and despair she heard in his voice to the dark recesses of her mind and focusing on Striker instead. "What do I have to do?"

"Simple. Drink this - but make sure you only take half. Any more than that and Davie will pay the consequences." He held the beaker out to her.

She stared at it. It was bubbling away, flecks of light sparkling in its depths. "You want to make sure it's safe. That you didn't make any mistakes following Gideon's notes."

"I didn't. But who's to say Gideon didn't make any errors? I'd rather not risk my life to find out - especially when I have yours to gamble with."

She reached out to grasp it, stopping when her fingertips were barely close enough to graze the glass. "Gideon was pretty smart, right? So there's a good chance this will work..."

Striker shrugged. "Only one way to find out." He shoved the beaker towards her, and her fingers instinctively wrapped around it.

She brought it closer, mesmerized by the way tiny motes of silver flashed in its depths. "If this works, I can be anything I want to..." She lifted the beaker up to her mouth. The formula smelled like a combination of pickled beets and milk of magnesia, but that didn't matter.

Not when she was so close to getting what she wanted.

"I could be a god," she whispered, tilting the formula towards her lips.

"Not so fast." Striker's hand shot out, wrapping around hers and stopping her from drinking. "You're a little too eager there. I don't want you getting any ideas. I'm the one in control here."

Cassie tightened her grasp, refusing to relinquish her hold. "Are you?" She grinned. "You're not as smart as you think you are, Striker. I seriously can't believe you handed me the formula. I barely even had to try." This close, she knew she could take him if she had to... but she might not have to. "The way I see it, you have two choices. You let go and let me drink the formula, and I might be gracious enough to leave you half. Or you can try and fight me, risking the beaker getting broken and neither of us getting what we want."

"You're bluffing." He shifted uneasily, moving his weight from the balls of his feet to his heels and back again. "You don't want it to break, either."

"Like you said, only one way to find out. So which one is it going to be?"

He relaxed his grip and she felt a moment's surprise. She hadn't thought he would take the sane way out.

Her surprise ended when he dropped his hand entirely, shifting away from her. "Neither." Darting towards David, he pressed his gun directly against the other man's temple. "Unless you want your first act as a deity to be raising him from the dead. 'Course, they never come back entirely right, do they? You should know that more than anyone." Eyes gleaming with madness, his finger tightened against the trigger, a hair's breadth away from pulling it the rest of the way.

"Don't," she breathed, hardly able to get

the word out past the tightness in her throat. Theoretically she'd known her plan would put David at some risk, but the difference between theory and reality was more than she was prepared for. "Don't do it. I won't get greedy again. I'll only drink half, I swear. I'll even pour it into separate containers so there's no way for me to double-cross you."

"If you think I'd trust you now, you're denser than I thought. I'll be taking the vial now."

"Here." Hands trembling, she held it out to him.

He snatched it away from her. "You blew your chance, sweetie. Now you can live with the results." He poured the contents of the vial into his mouth, gulping it down without a further breath.

Thank God. Now all she had to do was wait.

He stood triumphantly, empty vial in his hand and an arrogant smirk upon his face. "I think I will have you transform, after all," he said, crowing like a demented rooster perched atop a pile of dragon shit, thinking it made him cock of the roost. "But I'm going to be the one to decide what you change into. I'm thinking a geisha. A mute geisha."

Yeah, yeah. She was terrified. Well, she'd pretend she was anyway, for at least a few more seconds. *Thirty-three to be precise.*

"You wouldn't," she cried, dabbing at her eyes as she did her best to manufacture a few tears. "Please, don't!"

Thirty-one.

"Striker - no! She didn't do anything! Let her go!"

Damn. That was the worst part of the plan - not

being able to tell David there was no need to worry. She hated having to put him through so much pain and uncertainty.

Twenty-four seconds.

Striker was too far gone into his megalomaniac rant now - droning on and on about how he would rule the world and nothing could possibly stop him – to notice his distinct lack of transformation, so she allowed herself a small smile and silently tried to catch David's attention.

Nineteen seconds.

As she wiggled her fingers in a distinct "over-here" motion, David turned his gaze to her.

Seventeen seconds.

She couldn't tell him out loud; she didn't want to risk Striker hearing and using the gun in the last seconds he had remaining. So, she waited till David's eyes were locked on hers, and then closed one in a slow, indulgent wink.

It was enough.

He took a deep breath, and with it, his body relaxed, the muscles in his broad shoulders loosening until he appeared completely at ease.

"Just wait," she mouthed silently. *"Twelve seconds."*

He nodded.

Striker was practically foaming at the mouth now, intent on describing the ways he would get back at the people for all the imagined slights they had done to him.

Eleven seconds.

But like every other self-proclaimed criminal mastermind in the Post-Cataclysm world, Striker had a few fatal flaws.

Ten seconds.

The first was not remembering that deep down, almost everyone believes the good guys will *always* win.

Nine seconds.

The second was forgetting that masterminds *always* do something to mess themselves up.

Eight seconds.

And the third... was pissing Cassie off.

Seven seconds.

The gun he had been holding was long gone, dropped harmlessly to the ground sometime in the middle of his rant.

Six seconds.

His breathing had become labored - his chest heaving dramatically with each inhale and exhale.

It was time.

"Oh, Striker," she called, giving him her brightest smile, "there's something I forgot to tell you."

Five seconds.

"What," he muttered, looking at her with unfocused eyes, his lids heavy and drooping. What do you want?"

Four.

"I just wanted to tell you goodnight."

Three.

With a confused grunt, he collapsed to the

ground,

    Oh, shit. Two full seconds off? She was going to have to work on that for next time.

Chapter Nineteen

After shifting Striker's unconscious body to get better access to his belt, Cassie grabbed the keys to the handcuffs and rushed to David's side.

"How did you know that was going to happen?" he asked, rubbing his wrists to get the blood flowing back through them.

"It was easy." She helped him to his feet, his arm draped around her shoulder both for support and to remind herself that he was okay. "I switched out the polymer from Sasha's locket with a potion a friend's mom designed for me. I'm not sure exactly what's in it, but it nullifies the active ingredients of other chemical and magical compounds – and puts whoever takes it down for a nice, long nap."

"And the real polymer?"

"Is in a perfume bottle in my bag. I moved it from the locket after the lab took the other half. I wasn't sure what we would run into during our search, and I don't like to take unnecessary risks."

"Really?" His other arm snuck around her waist, pulling her face to face. "What if Striker hadn't changed his mind?" he asked, holding her tight. "He almost made you take half of it."

She settled into his embrace, relishing the reassuring solidity of him. "Not much chance of that. His ego's too big to let someone else get the glory."

"Still, there had to be a way that didn't put you in so much danger."

"Not without risking you," she said, embarrassed to admit how scared she'd been that he'd get hurt in the crossfire. "Anyway, it turned out okay in the long run."

"Thank God for that. I've never been so terrified as when I thought you were actually going to drink that crap." He shuddered, and she could feel the vibrations run through his body.

Shit. This wasn't going to be easy.

"Yeah... about that. I've been thinking... What if I did? Take the real one, I mean."

His eyes darkened. "Why would you want to do that?" he asked, sounding as if he were forcing the question through tightly clenched teeth.

"You know why." Admitting it was hard, but she owed him the truth. "I wasn't lying when I told Striker I wanted to use the formula. I know you don't believe in my curse, but it's real, and I want it gone." She bent down to rifle through Striker's backpack. "Striker has Gideon's notes somewhere in here, and with those and the real polymer, it will be easy."

"It's too dangerous."

"It might be if it got into the wrong hands, but we're the *right* hands. And after we're done, we'll destroy all the evidence so no one else can recreate the experiment." She dug through the bag, shifting around plastic beakers and assorted ammunition until she found what she was looking for. "Ah! Here they are." She pulled the papers out and riffled through them, crowing with excitement when she realized they were written simply enough for a non-scientist to be able to follow. "They're not even that complicated. It'll only take us a couple of minutes at the most." She stood up, papers in hand, anxious to grab the polymer from her own bag and begin the process.

"Don't." David's hand shot out to wrap around her wrist, halting her progress. "Don't do it."

"I have to."

"No, you don't," he said, gently tugging on her wrist. "There's nothing you need to change. Not for me. Not for anyone."

"I do." She tried to pull away from him, but he held tight. "You don't understand."

"Then tell me," he begged.

"It's easy for you to say everything is going to be okay, but it's not. This curse is turning me into someone I don't want to be." Before it had happened - before Drew had broken her heart - she had been confident. She'd been able to trust the people around her. She'd been able to trust her own judgment. But now... "Look at me, David... look at all the mistakes I've made on this case. I missed everything Striker was doing, I haven't helped Gideon find his peace, hell, I haven't even figured out who killed him. And all because I let myself get twisted into loops trying to figure what was going on between you and me. How much worse will it get before I finally put a stop to it?"

"You think I'm bad for you." His voice was pained, and his normally ruddy skin was pale. "That I've made things worse for you."

"No. It's not you: it's me. It's always been my fault. Obsessing over whether I can let myself be with you is bad for me. How can I do what I need to do if I'm constantly worried my heart's going to be broken? That's not who I am. That's not who I want to be."

"Then trust me."

"How can I when my curse is still looming over us?" She shook her head, tired of denying the truth. "I used to pretend it didn't matter, but it does. I want to be close to someone. I want to be close to *you*. If using Gideon's invention lets me do that, I'm willing to take the chance."

"I'm not."

"David..."

His fingers loosened, not to release her hand but to caress it instead. "You're perfect as you are. You don't need to change anything."

She found herself weakening. "Just the curse."

"No."

"Do you know how infuriating that is?" she asked, momentarily distracted from her goal by his sheer pig-headedness. "No one ever tells me no."

"I do. And there's no way I'm letting you take that formula."

"Oh, yeah?" she challenged. "What are you gonna do to stop it?"

He looked down at her and did the cruelest

thing she could have imagined. "Please…," he asked, his eyes open and unguarded, staring at her with more trust and concern than she had ever seen before. "For me."

She handed him the notes, not even bothering to argue when he pulled a lighter from the depths of his pocket and sent them up in flames.

Chapter Twenty

One thing the Cataclysm didn't do was to change how love worked.

***

Cassie packed her bags, carefully placing everything but the clothes she would wear for the flight home and the silk kimono she was currently wearing in a precisely arranged system. She wanted to have everything ready when it was time to leave tomorrow morning. She didn't want anything to slow her down. Not when it was taking all she had to force herself to leave.

She hadn't found Gideon, but it didn't matter. Gideon had never been a danger to those around him. He could find his peace in his own way and in his own time.

If only Cassie could find it as easily...

With the last suitcase fully packed, she started her nighttime routine. Teeth brushed... check. Face washed... check. Whiskey poured... she hesitated, glass in hand. She'd had her fill of mystical concoctions lately.

She set the whiskey glass back on her bedside table, leaving the bottle next to it unopened.

Maybe it wouldn't be so bad. She and David couldn't be together, but they could arrange to see each other every couple of years.

She could settle for that, couldn't she? If it was all she could have?

As she turned down the covers on her bed, the knock she had been dreading came at her door.

She'd known he wouldn't let her go without a fight, but she was terrified to let him in. Half of her wanted to scream at him for making this harder than it needed to be; the other half wanted nothing more than to pull him into her room and lock them both inside it, keeping them trapped in their own private world where her curse could never reach them.

She opened the door, unsure which half would prove triumphant.

David stood there, dressed in those damned faded jeans and a soft cotton shirt, and pleasure won decisively, crushing anger into miniscule pieces and setting them on fire.

"Hi," he murmured, resolutely focusing on her eyes and not the silky black kimono that ended only centimeters below her ass. "Can we talk?"

"It's pointless," she said, stepping aside to let him into the room anyway. "I've told you; I'm not going doing anything that might hurt you." It was the one thing she was sure of; no amount of temporary pleasure was worth her curse changing him.

"That's not something you have to worry

about." He moved towards her, resting his hands on her shoulders, looking so confident Cassie wanted nothing more than to agree with him. "The only way you could hurt me is if you say we can't be together." The warmth from his palms seeped through the thin fabric of her kimono. "Please..." he said, lowering his head until his forehead was resting against hers and his lips were only a millimeter away from grazing her mouth. "Just give me a chance."

Her hands lifted to his chest, resting on the chiseled plane. "No." It took all her willpower to push him away. "I'm sorry. I can't."

"I know I've given you reasons not to trust me, but I swear, I'll do better..."

"No... David... it's not that. I trust you. I do. And it's not because I don't want you, because I do. More than you could imagine."

"Then why? Why can't we be together?"

Cassie had thought long and hard about that very question. She'd examined it from every angle, hoping to find a different answer, but the outcome was always the same. If she let him into her life, her curse would change him, and she couldn't be responsible for that.

"Being betrayed by someone you love hurts," she said, staring at the ceiling so she didn't have to look him in the eyes when she admitted how she really felt. "It's one of the worst things you can imagine. Not only do you lose the one person who's supposed to care about you more than anyone else does, but you have to wonder why they could betray you so easily. No matter how much you try to quiet it, there's always this little voice inside your head telling you that you must have done something wrong to deserve being treated like that."

David reached out to take her hands in his. "Cassie... no." His fingers grazed over her wrists, the feel of his thumb gliding over her skin doing nothing to calm the pounding of her heart. "No one deserves for that to happen to them, but especially not you. You have to know that."

She closed her eyes, blocking out the tears that were threatening to spill down her face. "I do. Mostly, anyhow. The guilt creeps back in sometimes when I'm lying in bed alone and I can't fall asleep, but the rest of the time I can usually convince myself it's not my fault."

David's hands clenched around hers. "It's not. It's all on them, not you. Never you." She couldn't see him, but she could hear the pain in his voice.

Pain for her.

"It's okay," she said, rushing to reassure him, "it's really not that bad. I'm a pretty independent type of person anyway and I've gotten used to being alone... although now that I've met you, it's going to be considerably harder."

"Then don't do it." It was little more than a whisper, but it was filled with so much hope and desperation it felt like a physical blow to her heart. "Stay with me. Or let me come with you. I don't care as long as which as long as it means I can be near you."

Tears ran down Cassie's face. "I can't. Being

without you is going to be one of the hardest things I've ever had to do, but it would be a thousand times worse if I let myself be with you and ended up destroying you in the process." *It was the worst thing she could think of, worse than losing him, worse than never really having him in the first place.* "The guys I've been with before… what my curse did to them really wasn't that much of a change." She opened her eyes and stared at the blurred expanse of the ceiling as her head began to pound. "I've never had the best taste in men; I think they would have betrayed me even without the curse. But you… you're different. You're a good person. A good man." *No, not good. The best.* "If I change that… if I turn you into someone who could lie and cheat… I don't think I'm strong enough to be responsible for that."

David shifted his grip, sliding his hands up Cassie's arms as he gently tugged her towards him, pulling her into a warm embrace. "You won't have to."

"How can you say that?" Cassie asked, trying not to give in to the longing to sink further into his touch.

"You said it yourself," he said, one hand coming up to cradle her head against his chest. "Those guys weren't good enough for you. It would be different with us. Magic can't bring anything out of a person that isn't already there, and there is no way any spell or curse could make me do anything to betray you."

"You say that now, but you'll change." *She knew he would. They all did.* "No one is strong enough to fight it."

"I am." His fingers wove into her hair, rubbing little circles into her scalp and easing the pain of her headache. "Just give me a chance to prove it."

She could feel the steady pulse of his heart, steady and true, and she knew he believed what he was saying. "How can you be sure? How do you know I won't irritate you so much you'll be glad to get rid of me?"

His fingers stilled. "No matter how mad we get at each other - and I'm sure we will, especially if you keep being so reckless with your safety - it will never make me love you any less."

"You love me?" She raised her head. He was staring down at her with a look in his eyes just like the one that had confused her for so long - warmth and passion and tenderness all rolled up in one.

He nodded. "Since the moment we met. And... I think maybe you love me, too?"

"Yeah." She couldn't deny it. She might not know a lot about love, but she knew there was no other way to explain how she felt around him. "Yeah, I do."

"Good." He smiled, and it was like the sun had risen, kindling a warmth in Cassie's soul and setting her heart on flame. "It's settled, then."

"It is?"

"Of course. Love conquers all, right?" David's grin grew more dangerous, lighting his face with a hungry fire. "So maybe we should celebrate?" His hands moved down her shoulders, slipping down her arms to bracket her waist. "The question is how?"

"I could maybe think of a few suggestions. But… what if you're wrong?"

"What if I'm not?" he asked, his fingers pressing gently into the flesh at her hips, urging her closer to him. It was getting harder to concentrate on what she'd been worrying about as he started to work on the sash of her robe, gently tugging at the knot in an effort to release it. "Shouldn't we at least try to find out?"

"I want to." The knot gave up its meager resistance, and his warm hands slipped inside her robe, stroking her bare flesh and making her head spin. "But I don't know how."

"Believe in us… not your curse." His hands moved even lower, toying with the edge of her carefully color-coordinated silk underwear. "Do you think you can do that?"

"I think so." *If he kept touching her like that, she was willing to do anything.* "It'll be hard," she said, "but I think I can give it a shot." As she heard the words out loud, it came to her in a flash…

She was lying. To David and to herself. Trusting him had never been the problem. It was trusting *herself* that was difficult. Trusting whether or not she had the strength to risk her heart again. And if it meant the difference between having him in her life or having to say goodbye, there was no question what her answer was going to be.

She curled her fingers around his shoulders, pulling him even closer. "I believe in you," she said, her heart racing as she realized there was no doubt in her mind. "I believe in us."

Suddenly, a bright light erupted from her skin, enveloping Cassie in an unearthly glow as a strong gust of wind tore through the room, lifting her hair and swirling around her before dissipating slowly into nothingness, leaving behind a hint of sea breeze and a curious feeling of lightness.

What the hell was that?!

Before Cassie could ask the question out loud, David broke away from her with a stunned look on his face. "Was that what I think it was? Did you just have a spontaneous transformation?"

Cassie shook her head. "No. It couldn't be. I was born after the Cataclysm and inherited my parents' traits so it's unlikely I'd undergo a change of my own. And even if I was going to happen, I'm way past the time I would have done so. It only occurs during puberty or..." she drifted off as realization struck.

"...times of intense emotional and physical reactions. I can see how this qualifies." David ran his fingers through his hair, messing the dark brown strands up in a way that left Cassie longing to sink her own hands into them. "My God... I never thought I'd ever see one, and now for it to happen like this..." he trailed off, his soulful brown eyes wide with shock and a pale cast to his olive skin.

Cassie felt sick to her stomach. She'd known the world had a sick sense of humor, but this was carrying things too far. "David, I'm so sorry... It should have happened to you. You're the one who deserves a transformation. Maybe if we can figure out why it happened..." It must have been a delayed reaction to Gideon's formula. The lab results had said that the compound was ineffective, amounting to little more than highly carbonated soda water, but they must have made a mistake. "We'll have the lab re-run the test... I'm sure they can figure out how to trigger a transformation for you, too."

"Cassie, slow down." David laughed, catching her in his arms and holding her in a comforting embrace. "Please tell me you're not worrying because you changed and I didn't."

"You can't tell me you're not upset." He dipped his head, bending to kiss the spot where her neck met her collarbone, and she momentarily forgot what she was trying to say. "You... you've always wanted to go through a transformation... to find your purpose," she said when he momentarily paused his exploration and she regained her train of thought, "and if anyone deserves to find it, it would be you. But I got it instead."

He moved from kissing her neck to nibbling lightly at it and then soothing the effected area with his tongue. "Does it feel like I'm mad to you?"

No. Frankly, it felt... phenomenal.

"Uh... I don't think so," she mumbled with the little capacity for speech she still had. "Maybe you should keep doing that a little longer so I can be sure?"

"It would be my pleasure." True to his word, he doubled down on his efforts, his fingers joining in to trace their own meandering journey over her skin. "You see," he said, whispering the words as his lips began to follow the slow, tormenting path his fingers were forging, "you seem to be forgetting I already found my purpose. It's you, remember? And it's not as if I'm not benefiting from your transformation."

"You are? How?" *It's not like they knew what was different about her yet. If it wasn't a physical change – which this one didn't seem to be - sometimes it took days, if not months, to figure out what the transformation was.*

David lifted his head. "I think it's pretty obvious, don't you?" he said, staring at her as if the answer should be self-evident.

"Oh sure, of course... but maybe you could tell me anyway."

He laughed, straightening up to look her directly in the eyes. "Cassie, I'm going to need you to stop and think for a second." His hands, which had worked their way inside of her robe, shifted to her hips, resting lightly on either side. "What were we talking about right before your transformation happened?"

"That you loved me? And... that I loved you, too?"

He nodded, looking pleased. "Yes, and I'm never going to get tired of hearing that, but there was something else."

"There was?"

"Uh-huh. You were saying you believed in me. That you believed in *us*."

"So?"

"Transformations act on what you believe in the most, Cassie."

"Oh." *That... made sense when she thought about it. But if that's what the magic acted upon, then...* "Oh." Her cheeks reddened as she realized what he meant.

"Exactly." His hand tightened around her hips. "I don't think your curse is going to be a problem for us anymore, not when the world itself agrees you can trust in us." His hands began to move again, one sliding up to the middle of her back and the other dipping down to graze the lace at the top of her underwear.

She melted into the touch, but there was one little thing still bothering her. "You're probably right, but we still might have a problem. If transformations are triggered by heightened emotional and physical reactions..."

"Yes?"

"Does that mean one's going to happen every time we get naked?"

"There's only one way to find out, isn't there?"

Well, when he put it that way, there was really only one thing to be done...

She wrenched his shirt up, pulling it over his head and revealing the full magnificence of his chest. He was a work of art in any light and in any setting, but here in her room, lit only by a small bedside lamp and the fire burning deep within her heart, he was a masterpiece.

Not wanting to be outdone, he eased her underwear down then slid the robe off her shoulders, sending it sliding to the floor to land in a silken puddle.

"Anything else?" he asked, smiling so broadly she thought her heart might crack in two from the joy of it.

Maybe one more thing.

"I love you." The words came easy, rising from her heart and slipping out her lips without any of the fear and pain they had caused so many times before. "I just thought I should tell you again." Then she stretched up, threading her fingers through his thick, dark hair and tugging at it to bring him even closer.

He responded eagerly, claiming her mouth in a headlong rush as his hands explored her naked body, skimming over the smooth skin of her back and up to her shoulders before finally dipping into the valley between her breasts.

"David..." she moaned, unwilling to wait another moment now that last barrier between them had finally disappeared, "stop teasing."

"Patience," he relied with a wicked grin, "we have all night." He trailed his forefinger in an ever-diminishing circle around her nipple, coming closer and closer but never quite touching it.

"Forget all night," she said, biting at the rough underside of his jaw and savoring the salty taste of his skin. "I want you now."

"Far be it from me to deny my lady." His hands cradled her breasts, his thumbs running over the raised peaks and sending shafts of lightning to the core of her being. With exquisite care, he dipped his head and began to lave her with his lips and tongue, switching from one side to another in a slow, languorous rhythm.

Arching her back to offer herself more freely, Cassie's hands clenched on his shoulders, supporting herself as her legs grew weak underneath her. She didn't want him to stop, didn't want to do anything to halt the heady sensations coursing through her, but she wanted more. She wanted to touch him, too; she wanted to feel him everywhere.

As if sensing her hesitation, he raised up, his eyes burning with a smoldering question. Reading the answer on her face, he swept her up in his arms and carried her to the bed. Lying next to her, their bodies pressed tightly together, they sampled and tasted, each learning the other's likes and dislikes until they couldn't stand the wait anymore.

Covering her with his strong, muscled body, David moved between her legs, her ankles around his calves as she welcomed him with everything she had to offer.

"Are you sure?" he asked with a truly heroic - if completely unnecessary - degree of self-restraint.

Oh hell, yes.

Chapter Twenty-One

Cassie woke, snapping to instant awareness. Next to her, David's naked body lay half-uncovered by the sheets they had managed to thoroughly displace over the course of the last few hours. She could now personally testify that every inch of him was a work of art... and there were a lot of inches.

So why was she wide awake?

Maybe it had something to do with the tapping at the window.

She hopped out of bed, careful not to disturb her sleeping love - he had more than earned his rest. Pulling her robe on, she hurried to the window, reaching it just as another tiny little "ping" sounded. Looking out, she could see a dim figure standing several stories below, throwing pebbles up.

Gideon.

She signaled him, telling him to wait, and he nodded his head. Within minutes she was dressed and on her way outside. He was waiting where she had seen him, silent and stern, barely visible in the fog that swirled around him.

When she got up close, she wondered how she had ever gotten them confused. Gideon was harder than his brother, more brittle. He was missing the spark that made David... David.

"This was never about Striker, was it?" she asked, cutting straight to the heart of the matter. "It wasn't about your invention, either. Not really."

It had taken her too long to realize, but the last few hours had taught her something important. *The only thing truly worth coming back to life for was whatever – or whoever – had made it worth living in the first place.* She was willing to bet Gideon had learned that lesson, too.

"No." Gideon agreed, confirming her suspicions. "If I had realized the danger Striker posed to my family, I would have done something to stop him. Hell, I would have given him the formula... although it wouldn't have done him any good. I never did find the right polymer - I only told John it worked so he'd accept a bonus from me." He shrugged, and in the movement she could see more of a resemblance to his brother. "He needed the money," he continued. "He was planning on proposing to Sasha."

He really was similar to David. Both of them would do anything in their power to help someone in need. *Especially if it was someone they cared for.*

"So who was it?' she asked, needing to know the truth, both for her own curiosity and to give David and the rest of the MacDuff family some peace of mind. "It's obvious you know who your murderer is. You've probably known even before you got your hands on the mechanic's report." He wouldn't have stolen the report otherwise. "You weren't trying to *get*

282

information; you were trying to *hide* it."

Gideon flinched, his pale skin growing even more ashen until it was almost the same color as they grey haze surrounding them both. "It doesn't matter who did it."

"I think it does." He may not feel the need to pursue his murderer, but the law was another matter. "What if they do it to someone else?"

"She won't. She didn't mean to hurt anyone; it was an accident." His eyes, the same dark brown as David's but bloodshot and weary, locked on to Cassie's, begging her to believe him.

"How can you be sure?"

He held out his hand and a slim figure slipped out of the fog to stand at his side.

"Because," Nim said, reaching out to place her palm in his, "I have regretted what I did every second of every day since it happened. The car was supposed to stall before it left the mansion grounds. I just wanted him to stay... to spend some time with me." The trees nearby shivered in distress, creaking and groaning as tears ran down the wood nymph's face.

"No... don't cry, darling." Gideon looked at Nim, his face softening and regaining color until he looked almost human. "It was my fault. If I wouldn't have been so stubborn..." He turned to Cassie. "Before I died, I thought I didn't have time for love, that it could wait until I was ready. Nim tried to tell me what we had was too special to put on hold, but I didn't believe her..." He dropped his head, staring at the ground. "I came back to tell her she was right. She was right all along."

A week ago, even a day ago, Cassie wouldn't have understood what he meant, but now it made all the sense in the world.

"So, what now?" she asked. "Where do you want to go from here?"

Gideon raised his head. "Promise me you won't turn her in. Promise me she'll be safe after I die again."

"Gideon… no!" Nim pulled at his hand. "Don't say that! You're not going to die!"

"I won't turn her in," Cassie said, ignoring Nim's ever-increasing cries. "You have my word."

"Good." Gideon nodded, looking grimly satisfied. "Then I've done everything I needed to do; it's time for me to leave before it's too late." His sadness was etched on his face, highlighting the lines that distinguished him from his brother. "I know I can't go on like this," he said, waving his free hand to indicate his undead state. "I was hoping you could help me to go peacefully. Before I lose sentience and hurt someone for real."

"No!" Nim yanked his hand harder. "I lost you once. I'm not going to lose you again." She pulled at him again, trying to drag him back to her woods. "You'll be safe in the forest. I won't let anyone else in, so there won't be anyone who could get hurt even if you do forget yourself for a little while."

"I could hurt *you*, and I would never forgive myself if that happened."

"You wouldn't. You *couldn't*. It's not in your nature."

Cassie watched the two of them arguing; Nim so desperate to hold on to Gideon and Gideon so anxious to do anything to keep from harming her.

Oh, hell.

"Not that either of you has bothered to ask my opinion… but this whole thing is irrelevant. I have no intention of killing anyone tonight."

They both turned to Cassie, Gideon with surprise in his dark eyes and Nim with hope in her light ones.

"You're not?" she asked. "But isn't that why you came here?"

"No… I came here to find Gideon and see if he was causing problems. He's not, other than the fact that you're both keeping me from the man I love, who at this very moment is lying naked in my bed without – *and I cannot stress this enough* – me being there to appreciate it! So, here's what we're going to do. You," she said, wagging her finger in Gideon's undead face, "have a second chance to be with the woman you love, so quit being noble and listen to what your heart is telling you. You came back from the dead almost a year ago, and you haven't regressed into a brain-eating monster in all that time. I'm pretty sure that means you're not going to."

"And you," she said, switching her attention to the wood nymph, "No matter how much you love him, you can't be the only thing in Gideon's life. He's going to need all the support he can get. You both are. That means family dinners, game nights with friends, and, for heaven's sake, letting him go on the occasional business trip if it's called for."

"I... understand."

"I hope so, because any more tampering with cars or other homicidal tendencies and you and I will be revisiting that conversation about blowtorches we had a while ago."

"Never again," Nim nodded solemnly, eagerly clutching Gideon's hand. "I promise."

"Good. Then as far as I'm concerned, that's the way it's going to stay unless I hear you're trying to eat people's brains, okay? So don't eat anyone's brains."

"Okay?" Gideon answered with a confused look.

"Okay. Now I'm going back upstairs to sleep with my boyfriend, but I'll expect to see both of you at the main house for breakfast in the morning. Don't be late."

She marched back into the castle, storming into her room and slamming the door with a loud bang. "Honestly, some people make everything way more complicated than it needs to be."

"Cassie?" David groaned, awakened by her outburst. "What are you doing?"

"Just taking care of some business." She striped off her clothes and climbed into the bed next to him, breathing in the uniquely David-scent that made her feel like she had finally found her way home. "I'll tell you all about it in the morning. Oh, and we'll need some extra place settings. Your brother and Nim are going to be there."

"He is?" He paused in the midst of reaching for her, surprise and excitement evident in his voice.

"They are?"

"Yep." She snuggled closer to him, sighing in contentment when his arms closed the rest of the way around her. "In fact, I have a feeling we're going to be seeing a lot more of them." Of their own accord, her arms worked their way around him, curling around to caress his back and savor the feel of him.

He bent his head to place a kiss on her bare shoulder. "That's great," he said, punctuating his words with alternating bites and kisses to her throat. "But breakfast is an awfully long time away. Do you think we'll be able to find something to keep occupied till then?"

"I believe we will."

And they did.

Coming Soon

Read on from an excerpt from another exciting story set in the World of the Cataclysm.

∞∞∞

A saxophone solo crept through the smoky air, reaching out with tendrils born of shattered dreams and unfulfilled longing. It carried with it the scent of cloves and cinnamon, invoking long-forgotten memories of girlish childhood dreams and sunny days spoiled by unexpected storms. All that was missing was the taste of a lover's Judas kiss, a taste of sweet molasses gone sour.

Throw in that, and I'd be stuck in the perfect menage a trois of misery, a trifecta of heartbreak to haunt my senses and scar my soul.

A disembodied voice floated across the table, emerging from somewhere in the depths of a robe darker than the inside of a sinner's nightmare. "It's all in there." Pushed by an invisible hand, an envelope slid across the table, its heavy manila paper leaving trails in the sad remains of spilled whiskey. "His name, where you can find him, even what kind of aftershave he wears when he's human."

In all the time I'd known the creature sitting across from me, I'd never seen what was inside of that robe. I didn't want to. For what I was about to do, I wanted the cool comfort of anonymity.

Against my will, I found myself reaching for the envelope, tracing the seam of its sealed flap and memorizing the pebbly feel of its innocuous exterior under the pads of my fingers.

"And when he's not human? What does he wear then?"

The robe shifted, threatening to gap open and reveal a glimpse of its enigmatic inhabitant, but the overhead lights flickered and shadows leapt in to cloak its true form. "He's a lion."

A lion, huh? I'd never gone after one of those before, and for good reason.

I took a hit of my bourbon. Its golden fire slid down my throat and began to drown my better judgement.

"I didn't think that would be a problem for you," the robe continued in a voice dry as a skeleton's sense of humor. "You've taken out wolves, panthers, tigers. Rumor has it you've even taken out a bear."

For once, rumor had it right. I had taken them all out – and look what it had gotten me. A room full of worthless trinkets and a head full of bad memories.

"It's not a problem… but were-lions cost more."

An unearthly chuckle spewed from the robe, and I found myself in sudden need of a bigger glass of bourbon.

"As always," he managed to say when his infernal cackling crawled to a pained stop, "money is negotiable."

Maybe for him; not so much for me.

"I'm sure we could work out something that would be mutually beneficial to us both."

I wanted to get up and walk away from the table, to forget things like him even existed, but something kept me rooted to my seat, something other than the sticky substance tacking my heels to the floor.

The robe and I both knew I didn't have a choice. I had to do this.

But I didn't have to do it gracefully.

"If I take this on, it had better be the last one. I want out of this game."

Even without a body, the robe managed to convey a sense of nonchalance, a casual shrug of non-existent shoulders. "If you don't want to do business, I'm sure I can find someone else who is interested. As you said, were-lions are in high demand. And this one's fur would look particularly nice lying on the floor in front of a fireplace." The cuff of the robe surged forward, making a feint at retrieving the dossier.

"Not so fast." My own hand shot out, claws lengthening to razor-sharp points and pining the envelope to the table. "I didn't say I wasn't in… I just said that this is it. I can't afford to keep doing this."

A satisfied hiss came from the depths of the hooded cowl. "Of course. I guarantee you won't have to take out any others after this one. So, it is agreed?"

"It's agreed. Ten thousand now, and another ten thousand if it takes." I slid my money towards him, the last little piece of my prodigal daughter's portion disappearing faster than a virgin in Valhalla.

The matchmaker rose, revealing an emptiness that somehow contrived to look smug and satisfied. "I wish you well, but I'll hate to see you go. You were one of my best customers."

I can imagine. It's not everyone who will go to these lengths to get a blind date for an ex's wedding.

Acknowledgements

To my husband, with whom I have been living my very own love story.

To my three wonderful children, who are growing into amazing adults who I am exceedingly proud of.

To a phenomenal group of friends who put up with me and all of my writing neuroses. Janet, Megan, Treva, Carie, Christy... love you all.

To my brother Jim, a great advisor who also happens to be a fantastic writer.

To everyone who has contributed in any way to the production of this book.

And, last but not least, thank you to all the wonderful readers who have been kind enough to give this story a chance. Without you, none of this would have been possible.

About The Author

Cameo Macpherson

Cameo MacPherson is a pen name for Cathy Greco, a writer with a strange sense of reality. She honestly thinks it's possible to pursue a writing career, raise three children, and fight off an encroaching zombie horde all at the same time. (Although sometimes she does get the children and the zombies confused.)

A graduate of St. Vincent College in Pennsylvania, Cathy is proud to have put her degree in Advertising/Communications to absolutely no use, and hopes to continue doing so.

She can be found on Twitter and Instagram @cameomacpherson, on Facebook @CatherineGreco, and on Tiktok @cameomac

Books By This Author

Dead In Bed

Become a princess… check. Find a handsome prince… Check? Survive a horde of angry zombies… wait, what?!

A lighthearted fairy tale romance now with 20% more zombies.

Thistle; By Cathy Greco

Thistle is a fairy, but her life is anything but magical. She's an Unwanted - useful only for serving her superiors. She'll prove she's capable of more, though… no matter the cost.

A YA Fantasy for anyone who feels like they don't belong

Made in the USA
Monee, IL
12 May 2024